SISSY MAID
IN THE MIRROR:

SISSY MAID
IN THE MIRROR:

A sissy maid missy sister series, part two

M MISSY

To order additional copies of this book, contact:
Xlibris Corporation
1-888-795-4274
www.Xlibris.com
Orders@Xlibris.com
115701

CONTENTS

A LOOK BACK AT:

SISTER, SPANKINGS, SISSY MAID.

A sissy maid missy sister series, part one

Introduction,

The Paddle and the Hairbrush,

My Sister's First Spanking,

My Second Hairbrush Spanking,

My First Witnessed Spanking,

Punching, Spanking, Humiliation,

My Sister's Second Spanking,

Lucy and Joey,

Swim Club,

Jill's Spanking,

A LOOK INSIDE:

SISSY MAID IN THE MIRROR

A sissy maid missy sister series, part two

My sister, Jill, and I were headed to college in September and I would actually be on my own for the first time in my life. Both scary and exciting I thought.

However, it sure did not turn out the way I envisioned it to be. NOT EVEN CLOSE!

Some of the highlighted chapters below;

Introduction,

Missy ??????????

Preparing for College,

The House,

Meeting the B.I.T.C.H.S.,

Missy's Sissy Maid Training Begins,

College Classes,

Cleaning Duties,

Tuesday's Housework,

Wednesday's Housework,

Spanking,

The Dry Cleaners,

Standing in the Corner

Mom takes Missy Shopping,

Sissy Maid Practice,

Miss T's Fine Ass,

The Door Bell,

The Dry Cleaners, Missy's in Trouble,

Oh! My, the Big Thick Strap,

Lick What??????

Missy Humiliation,

Sissy Maid Test,

Home Alone,

INTRODUCTION:

Hello, my name is Jack and this is the story of how I became sissy maid missy.

My twin sister, Jill, and I grew up in the suburbs of Philadelphia in the 50's and 60's. Yes, we are Jack and Jill. My parents thought that was funny. However, everyone seems to remember us that way, both Jill and I have come to enjoy it was well.

The first 12 years of my life were so nondescript that I really do not remember most of it. I just went to school, a Catholic grade school, played with the neighborhood kids, mostly sports, and watched TV.

As far as discipline in the family, both my sister and I had received a two or three hand spankings before we turned 12, but they were nothing to remember as they did not seem like a big deal. After all, we were just young kids and could not get into very much trouble.

However, our mother did teach us to obey her mostly by having us stand in the corner. Our mother basically gave us a choice, we could either obey her promptly and without an argument or we could stand in the corner and then obey her later. It was always up to us.

From an early age Mom practiced teaching us to obey. Obey the first time, obey without an argument, and even obey without making unhappy faces. It did not matter was the instruction was, it was yes Mom, and you went to do it.

Mom would say it's time for your bath and I would say; can't I watch one more show? No! You can go and stand in the corner. 30 minutes later, Mom would say now it's time for your bath and all she would hear from me then was, yes Mom.

Jack, it's time to do your homework, OH MOM, can't I do it later. After 30 minutes of standing in the corner, Jack it's time to do your homework, yes Mom.

One of Mom's rules was that my sister and I were not allowed to fight and I don't mean physically really, rather verbally was the case most often. Mom expected a peaceful house. If my sister and I started yelling at one another it was 30 minutes in the corner for each of us and then Mom would ask if we were ready to play nice, yes Mom.

I found out later that our Mom was really smart in a way. I always thought that we needed to play well together as Mom liked a quiet and peaceful home. But, I found out later that she was trying to teach us to figure out how to get alone with one another because that would help us later in life to get alone with others.

It did not take too many times of standing in the corner before we figured out that it was better for us just to keep our mouths shut and obey Mom the first time then to have to stand in the corner first.

It was not like disobeying Mom or arguing with her ever produced any worthwhile results for us anyway. In the end we always ended up doing what she told us to do. So basically our house was governed by our mother and we were very well behaved kids who were very obedient.

As Jill and I went to a catholic school the nuns treated us the same way, so I also spent some time standing in the corner in school learning to be obedient to the nuns as well. Obedience seemed to be the only rule that needed to be learned in my life. If I was simply obedient I never got into trouble doing anything.

As I got older, maybe later in my 11th year and in my 12th year it seemed that I was spending more time in the corner than ever before. That did not seem true for my sister. Jill seemed to get in less and less trouble all the time and that was especially true in school.

At home, Mom was very consistent and it seemed like she never missed an opportunity to make me stand in the corner. Mom thought that if she was even a little bit lenient with me that I would start to think that I could get away with stuff sometimes and then I would misbehave to "test the waters" so to speak, then maybe I would even lose my fear or respect for her authority.

One of her rules was that we had to do all of our homework first thing when we got home from school. I wanted to go out and play when I got home from school. So I thought if I did some of my homework and then went out and play, that I could do the rest later by telling her that I forgot some. But as soon as I pulled out a school book after I was out playing, it was off to the corner for 30 minutes and then I could do the homework.

So to outsmart Mom, the next time I pulled that trick, I just forgot to do my other homework all together and I tried to get it done early the next morning in school before the teaching really began.

I got away with it a few times and then I was caught by one of the nuns who called Mom and I had to stand in the corner for 30 minutes on Friday, again on Saturday, and again on Sunday without being able to go out and play at all. As you could imagine, I gave up trying to fool Mom about my homework and did it right after I got home from school as she wanted us to, as least for a while.

As I got older and noticed girls somewhat, I started to talk to the girls a lot in school. However, the nuns did not think that was such a good idea. I had no idea why they felt that way but they did. The nuns were not any fun at all.

Anyway, every time we were caught it was off to the corner for both of us. After a while the girls did not want to talk to me because I kept getting them into trouble. However, I kept trying to talk to them as I got bored easily in school.

The boredom problem was a bigger problem for me which also explained why I talked to the girls so much. You see, unlike the other kids I learned very quickly, once the teacher said sometime and I heard it, I knew it. So when the nuns would backtrack and go over and over and over the same stuff again and again for the other kids I was totally board as I already knew that stuff.

So I tried to find something else to do, like talk to the girls. Or look out the window, or draw pictures of the nuns. The nuns really did not like that because

I would draw them like cartoon caricatures with giant heads or little heads and big bodies. They especially hated the one that I drew with the nun with huge breasts and little stick legs. There was just no pleasing those bitchy nuns.

It was not that I had forgotten about what Mom spent the 1st 12 years of my life teaching me, which was to simply to obey, obey, and obey some more. It just seemed that I would not think about that and would just react to my boredom at the time.

That would be except those times when I thought I was smarter than everyone else and could get away with something. But that never seemed to work out the way I expected. However, for some stupid reason, I kept trying.

So then Mom decided that if I got in trouble in school that she would repeat that in school punishment at home. So every time I spend 30 minutes standing in the corner I school, it was 30 minutes in the corner at home later that day as well. That actually was working and I was getting into much less trouble in school.

Then Jill and I turned 13 and everything changed.

After our thirteenth birthday any time we disobeyed Mom or broke any of her rules we

got our spankings with a hard wood hairbrush
and no longer just Mom's hand.

Over the first five years of the "hairbrush
era", Jill was spanked only 6 times. That
was not a lot over 5 years. Jill turned
out to be such a confident and responsible
young lady. I was even impressed with her.
Mom taught her well and Jill learned well.

Over that same five years, I was spanked
13 times and I was caned the last time for
a total of 14 times. However, that was only
three times per year, so I did not think I
was a really bad kid. I was never punished
when I did not deserve to be punished, so I
have to admit that I did earn every one of
those spankings.

As Jill and I were ready to go to college
and start a new chapter in our lives, I can
tell you this about how Jill and I were
raised by our parents.

Understanding that the first job of a
parent is to protect their children and
teach their children to be responsible
adults, what could I say?

Our parents did the best job that a
parent could do. Both Jill and I are the
most loving and most obedient and smart and
most responsible kids any parent could ever
want. We did not drink, gamble, sniff glue,

smoke, take dope, or get pregnant. However, we both did get great marks in school.

I am proud to tell you that I turned out to be the most respectful and loving and nice son any parent could ask for. Yes, and obedient too.

Never once did I ever think that my Mon was mean to me or too hard on me. My Mom did what she had to do to get me though those growing years that were so much trouble for many of my friends.

If you did not read my first book which covered all of mine and Jill's spankings, as well as, my Mom introducing me into the world of being her sissy maid as additional punishment, you can read;

SISTER, SPANKINGS, SISSY MAID
A sissy maid missy sister series, part one

Looking back on all the pain and embarrassment and humiliation or the hairbrush era I can say that I appreciated my Mom for caring enough to be my Mom and not my friend when I needed a Mom. Mom was my friend the rest of the time and a good friend at that.

Jill and I get along better than any other siblings we know. Jill and I truly care about one another and understand our perspective roles in our growing up process together.

As a result, Jill got me a room in the same house she and a few friends rented as their own personal college dorm. How great was that going to be, me and five college girls in the same house, without Mom to boss me around or to punish me. My punishment days were coming to an end. Me and five College girls in the same house! I could not wait!!!!!!!!!!

MISSY????

For those of you that may not know what a SISSY MAID is, a SISSY MAID

According to Wikipedia, is;

A male who cross dresses and adopts hyper-feminine behaviors and engages in stereotypical feminine activities, such as housekeeping, putting on makeup and often within the context of BDSM.

As it turned out that pretty much described the maid part of my life, the missy part of my life, which overall I really enjoyed more and more all the time.

A sissy will typically assume the submissive role to a dominate female and or male partner. Often sissy's also identify with other fetishes and sexual practices.

Being the submissive one was nothing new to me as I had been completely submissive

to my Mom and my sister for the last five
years of my life.

A sissy may be entirely heterosexual and
or bisexual and only desire to be dominated
by women, while other sissy's might be
bisexual or homosexual and desire to be
dominated by men. Then, others may desire
to be forced by his female partner to engage
in sexual acts with men.

I had no real experience with sex yet,
so I had no clue how the sex part was going
to turn out for me. In fact, I had no idea
that there would be any sex. I thought that
missy would just be a maid.

However, I was not a virgin as I had sex
with two girls so far in my young dating life.
However, we just had clumsy intercourse. As
I said, we were just finding our way with
sex at that point in my life.

The activities the sissy maid is made
to perform may range from mundane house
work tasks that a real maid would perform
to degrading tasks that invoke erotic
humiliation.

I knew all about the house work, but had
no clue as to the degrading and or erotic
humiliation that was coming my way.

Nevertheless, my own shorter definition of sissy maid MISSY is to say that MISSY had become a sexy French maid and submissive whore.

PREPAIRING FOR COLLEGE:

Looking forward to September, my sister, Jill, and I were scheduled to go to college. Just thinking about going to collage for me meant that I did not need to obey my Mom any longer and even better, that I did not need to obey my sister any longer.

Yes, I know that I thought the same things earlier in the year when I turned 18. But, now, I was going to be out of the house and away from Jill and my Mom and would not need to worry about being punished by them anymore.

However, I did wondered if I would remember everything my Mom taught me about my behavior or if I would just do whatever I wanted? I felt like I would be the same good kid? However, I really did not know how that I would react once I was free from my required female obedience.

For the first time in my life I would be on my own and not having a women or even a girl pushing me around anymore. Yes, I know that I had that long chat with my mother about being on my own, but I still felt that way anyway. Nevertheless, I will always keep my Mom's opinion in mind as I go on to my new life of being on my own and being in charge of myself.

Now, having thought those thoughts, it sounds like I am being unfair to my Mom. The truth is and has always been that I loved my Mom and I never really thought that she did anything wrong raising me the way she did.

In fact, I turned out to be a very well adjusted young man who never took drugs, did not smoke, did not drink, and never got into any trouble of any significance. I also knew that my Mom was always right.

It seemed very strange, compared to what I learned from other kids, that I had to obey my sister and take spankings from my sister and be embarrassed and humiliated in front of her friend, Beth. However, as I said; I turned out real well, better than almost all the kids I knew.

Most of my friends were not going off to college and would just be getting lower paying jobs. I'm not saying there was anything wrong with working with your hands, or not going to college. It's just that you can make more money working with your brain.

Anyway, I spent the first weeks of summer playing tennis, baseball, and swimming like I did every summer. The whole time I felt so free that I would soon be out from under my Mom's and my sister's authority.

No more humiliating spankings from my sister. No more of my sister pushing me around, no more being my sister's maid. Although, being my sister's maid never really bothered me. But, I still seemed to feel good about being free from her in September.

About three weeks into summer vacation, my dad asked me one day if I decided where I was going to stay when I went to college. The collage was a couple of hours from the house, too far to commute.

I told my dad that I guess I forgot to think about it and asked him for his advice. My dad told I had two choices, to stay in some small dormitory with a bunch of other guys and get a job to help pay for my needs besides the tuition which was paid for by my parents.

I really did not like the dormitory idea as I did not like crowds and parties and noise, but I figured I had no other choice.

Then my Dad added, the second choice was to go and talk with my sister as she may be able to help as we were going to the same collage, or should I be snooty and call it a university. Well, actually, it was called a university, not that I knew the difference if there was a difference.

Anyway, the next day when I saw my sister I told her about my discussion with Dad and asked her where she was going to stay. My sister told me that she made arrangements to rent a big old house a couple of miles from the campus out in the woods where it was real quiet and private.

I asked her how she could afford to rent a house. It was not like she had a job or anything close to a job. My sister told me that she made arrangements to rent most of the rooms out to other collage girls.

Jill told me that she would be collecting enough rent to cover all the household expenses and all of her personal expenses so that she would not have to get a job at all. Well, I guess my sister was pretty smart after all.

I told Jill that was really a good idea, but I did not think I had enough time to do the same thing before school started and she told me that I did not that she started planning this months ago. So I told her that I guess that I have no choice but to stay in the dorm.

Well, my sister said, maybe not. There was one part of the equation that she had not worked out yet which was the housework. She said that all the girls come from rich families and were paying top dollar for rent and expected to have all the housework done for them as they are use to having maids.

Jill said that she would have to do it as a last resort, but that was not her plan. So Jill said; if I wanted to come and do all the housework for everybody, I could stay on the top floor as it had not been rented as of yet.

There would be no cost to me in exchange for the housework and I would get food as well. Jill added that she even had some extra rent money to give me some cash so that I would not need to get a job outside the house. Well, that sounded like a good deal to me, I would be much happier living out privately in the woods then in some cramped dormitory.

I took the deal and then Jill said there is just one problem. What may that be I asked? Everybody who is staying there is a girl and we all agreed that boys are not allowed as we did not want to have any such distractions.

So, Jack, if you want to live there you will need to dress in your maid's clothes, as you do at home now, to do all you're cleaning. Otherwise, you have a private entrance in the back of the house and you can come and go as a boy without being in the main part of the house with any of the girls. Jack, you would also need to wear a wig and makeup so you look more like a girl.

As strange as that offer was, I accepted it right away. The real truth was that I did not mind dressing like a girl, if fact I actually enjoyed it and that way I could continue to do so.

Additionally, doing the housework sounded better to me then getting a job somewhere else. Although, not giving much thought about it at that minute, being dressed as a maid in front of those strange girls did seem embarrassing, I guess we will see.

THE HOUSE:

Jill rented a very nice house. You can see
it on the cover of the book. As far as I
was concerned it could not have been more
perfect. When you come in the front door
you have a very large living room on the
Left side with a TV and a fire place. On
the right side there was a bedroom with its
own bath.

   Down the hall on the left is a bathroom
and then an office which was next to the
outside patio. There were two French doors
that open onto the patio. On the right side
of the hallway after the guest bedroom was
a large dining room followed by a very large
kitchen.

   Going up the stairs from the first floor
to the second floor there was a very wide
hallway down the middle covering the entire
length of the house from the front to the
back.

Starting at the front of the house there is a set of windows overlooking the front greeting porch. For those of you not familiar with the greeting porch, in the old days when someone would come to visit it was customary for the lady of the house to go out on the second floor front small porch to greet them.

I think it was more of a safety issue as the women of the house did not want to be face to face with strange men that may have come to the home. From the second floor balcony she was safe, yet she could still see who was there and speak with them.

When the house was modernized, they removed the double doors to that porch and replaced them with windows. If you look at the picture on the cover you will see the porch with no access due to the window installation.

Down the hallway to the back of the house, the hallway leads to double French doors exiting to a large wood patio deck. The interior stairs were in the back part of the hallway by the double French doors and were also very wide like they built them in the old days, not thin staircases like they build today.

The rear wood deck also had a set of stairs that would go down to the parking lot in the back of the house.

There are 6 bedrooms and 4 bathrooms on the second floor. Beginning in the front of the house there were four bedrooms two on each side of the hallway, with a bathroom in between each set of two bedrooms, so each of those two bathrooms were shared by two rooms each.

At the back end of the hallway were two very large bedrooms, one on each side of the hallway, which were almost twice the size of the other two bedrooms and each of those bedrooms had a private larger bathroom.

Those two larger bedrooms each had double French doors leading to the 2nd floor large wood deck. The ladies who had those two rooms could actually come and go thru the French doors for entry and exit with not coming into the other parts of the house by the use the wood deck stairs.

The 3rd floor, where I was to live, had severely sloped ceilings due to the shape of roof, with only dormer windows. However, that area apparently was constructed for a maid or some type of servant as it not only had its own bathroom but had a small kitchen as well.

The washer and dryer were also on the 3rd floor making it convenient for the maid to do laundry without being in the main part of the house.

Last the 3rd floor also had an outside wood deck separated by the living room with one French door. The deck had stairs that went all the way down to the driveway so the maid could come and go without ever being in the main part of the house. So, that was very convenient as well as private for me.

Additionally, as Jill told me, in my case, none of the other girls were to see me as a male, so that was a perfect set up for me. When I went into the main part of the house, I would be dressed as the maid. When I was dressed as a male, I could come and go without coming into the main part of the house where the girls could see me.

The basement was all one big open space and also had a bathroom. There was an exit door so you could enter or exit to the parking lot. You could also enter and exit from the basement without being in the main part of the house as well.

If you came in from outside and you wanted to clean up you could go in thru the basement and do so before coming up to the main floors. The basement also had some weight lifting equipment and other exercise equipment.

Last, the basement had some strange looking hooks and cables attached to the rafters and I was not sure of their use. There was also

a TV and several couches and lounge chairs
and tables and even a refrigerator.

   In the back of the house there was a very
large old garage, I suppose at one time
they used it as a barn to keep horses and
or other farm animals. It was now used as a
garage and could hold 8 cars.

   The entire house has been modernized with
electric heat with a thermostat in room and
central air condition.

MEETING THE B.I.T.C.H.S.

We all moved into the house the Saturday or Sunday a week before classes started and everybody got to meet everybody. Of course when they met me I had to be dressed in my maid clothes, a black silk blouse and a black flared short tennis skirt with a white silk apron, white stockings and my 5 inch black high heels.

Jill also got me a wig and helped me learn to put on makeup. Not a lot of makeup, just some eye shadow, some red stuff on me cheeks, and some lip stick. When Jill was finished with me I looked in the mirror and thought that I did not look all that bad. I actually liked the sissy maid I saw in the mirror. In fact, for some reason, I got an erection looking at the sissy maid in the mirror.

Jill introduced me to;

Beth, you know Beth from our childhood, yes the same Beth that Jill and I grow up with, the same Beth that was my sister's best friend. Beth grew into a nice looking 18 year old girl with long brown hair, about 5'6" tall, had nice looking legs, average sized breasts, and had a very nice ass. Beth had a great smile and I thought prettier than most girls.

Ida, I think she was Jewish, not that it mattered. Ida was very short. About 5"2" tall with short athletic legs, not very sexy legs, but she did have large muscular thighs. Ida had short brown hair that had no style and just sort of hung off her head and she wore glasses. Ida did have a great looking ass however, but only had small breasts. Overall, Ida's only attractive feature was her ass. She did not even have a nice smile nor did she seem to smile very often.

Tara was a nice looking black girl. Tara was two years old then everybody else as she was a junior and not a freshmen like the rest of us, so she was about 21 years old. I think she was part black and part Latino. Tara had very nice long black hair. Tara was about 5'10" tall with nice long legs, average size breasts and had a real nice ass too. Overall, Tara was a real beauty, with a great smile.

That was the first time I was really around a black girl as where I grew up there were no black people. However, that did not bother me at all. Tara was as good looking as anyone else in that house as far as I was concerned. I would date her if she was not so much older and taller than me.

However, I never thought that Tara would ever date me. There was just something about Tara. Tara seemed to be extra classy and extra ladylike. Tara just gave off an air of superiority that I could not explain.

Jill, my sister, really turned out to be a very good looking young woman. She was about my height 5"8" tall with long brown hair, very nice large breasts, very nice sexy legs, and a nice plump ass also.

Overall, I think my sister, Jill, was the best looking of the group. Of course, except for Tara, maybe. Tara, being black, gave her a real different look but I still thought she was just as good looking as Jill.

However, Tara seemed to have a nicer ass. I realized as I was checking over those girls that for some reason I seemed to be most interested in the girl's asses, more so than the size of their breasts.

Cathy was about as normal and plan looking as a girl could be. Cathy was not bad looking nor was she good looking. Cathy was not tall nor was she short. Cathy did not have any body parts that were really nice, not a great ass, nor great tits, or real nice legs.

Cathy had medium length brown hair that was not real shinny and nice, but did not look bad either. Cathy did not have a nice smile, but her teeth were straight. Cathy was about as average as a girl could be.

Heather, she was a very nice looking long blond haired beauty. Heather was about as good looking as my sister only in the blond category. Heather was about 5"9" tall with really nice long sexy legs, nice full breasts, but Heather did not have as nice as an ass as some of the others did, she looked rather flat in the back.

Last and sadly for her, not the best, but the worst, was Sandy.

Sandy was Latino and about 5'4' and had short light brown hair, short stubby legs, very small breasts, but did seem to have even a nice plump ass. Even her face was less than average. Even Sandy's smile was not very nice.

Overall, I was to get to live with three beauties, Tara, Beth, and Heather. There was my good looking sister, but she did not count as she was my sister. The other three Sandy, Cathy, and Ida were nothing to look at. How lucky was I? Better than a dorm full of guys, NO?

However, I also realized that if you put all of the first letters of each of their first names in a line and you have B.I.T.C.H.S. I was hoping that that was just funny and not a future sign of our relationships to come.

All the girls realized that I was just a guy dressed in girl's clothes and that seemed fine with them as long I did everything they wanted.

However, one of the girls, Tara said; that I was unacceptable as I was and that I needed to feminize to look more act and move like a real girl instead of a guy in girls clothes. The rest of the girls told Tara that was fine with them and that Tara could do anything she wanted with me.

I was not sure what Tara meant except that maybe she wanted me to wear a different wig or more makeup or something and that was alright with me. At my age I had no understanding of what a cross dresser really was, but I did know from an early age that I got excited wearing my sisters short skirts and that I enjoyed dressing as the maid for my mother and sister over the past few years.

If you remember from my first book, my Mom made me wear those maid clothes and clean the house whenever I got a spanking or was otherwise being punished. So I had no problem if Tara wanted to help me look more like a girl, in fact, I liked the idea.

My sister, Jill, and Tara started to whisper to each other for a minute or two and them Tara looked at me and told me that I was to meet her that night at 6 pm to begin my training.

I did not know what Tara meant by training, but I was there to be the maid and if she wanted me to learn how to clean or do laundry or look more like a girl it was alright with me.

However just then, Tara stood up and came over to me and put her hand up under my very short skirt and felt my cock thru my panties. I could not believe that Tara did that right there in front of everyone, but she did. Nevertheless, Tara did find a fully engorged cock pressing against her hand. Tara just looked at me and smiled and said I thought so.

Before 6 pm came along I had an opportunity to speak with Jill and asked her about Tara. My sister told me that as Tara was two years older than all the other girls and has a lot of experience with maids. So, everyone voted that she would be in charge of me.

Tara was a junior and therefore will only be there for two years and then someone else would take over for the last two years. I

asked my sister if that was alright with
her as I was thinking that I would have
preferred my sister to be in charge of me
as I was use to her and know what to expect
from her.

However, Jill, told me that she thought
it was best as she would always have a
conflict of feelings if there were any
problems between me and one of the other
girls.

That made sense to me as well. Jill told
me to just do what Mom has taught me to do
for the past 18 years. That was, to obey the
women in my life. Jill told me to just obey
Tara and everything should be fine. After
all, Jill added, how hard could that be?

MISSY'S SISSY MAID TRAINING BEGINS:

I met Tara wearing my maid outfit at 6 pm in her room. The first thing Tara had me do was turn around so she could get a better look at me from all sides.

Tara told me that first, I will call her Miss T from then on and to address all of the other girls the same way. Everyone will be Miss and the first initial of their first name. Even you sister Tara said; you will only call her Miss J. Understand? Yes, Miss T.

However, Miss T continued; if I was just answering a question or acknowledging an instruction, then I could just say, yes Miss, as that particular person would know to whom I was speaking.

The second issue was my maid name. As I was apparently two people, I need to have separate names, one for each of me. I was allowed to keep my real name, Jack. However, my maid name was to be missy, maid missy.

Miss T noted that she liked that I was nicely shaved and asked if only shaved my legs or was by groin and ass shaved as well and I told Miss T that I was shaved all over except for my head and Miss T was happy to hear that and told me to keep that up.

Miss T said the next issue was obedience. Miss T told me that she expected complete obedience and not only to her but to all the girls. Understand? Yes, Miss.

Missy, let me cover obedience a little more for you. Missy, first of all, we really only have one week to teach what you need to learn before school starts and I realize that is not very much time.

So, to keep things very simple for you missy. You will be told what to do. You will say, yes Miss, and then you will obey.

Missy, should you do anything else, you will be punished.

Miss T told me that the only exception would be if I did not understand the instruction. Then I was to say, yes Miss and then I was to ask permission to speak. After I was given permission to speak, I was to ask my question. Once you're my question was clarified, I was to again say yes Miss again and then obey.

Can I be any clearer than that for you Missy? No Miss. Good missy, than let us move on.

I spent the last 5 years of my life obeying my Mom and my sister so obeying was something I was use to and that did not seem to be a problem for me. In fact, in some ways I liked it that way as I found it easier to just do what I was told to do then to be free to do was I wanted, or, to be wondering if I was making the correct decision.

Almost every time in my life so far that I got myself into trouble it was because I did what I wanted to do instead of either being obedient or asking permission to do something.

Miss T continued to tell me that she was fully aware of my upbringing by my mother and sister with corporal punishment and that would be the same in this house.

Miss T told me that neither my sister nor she would hesitate to punish me for any lack of obedience on my part. I was unhappy to hear that part as I thought that when I went to collage that I would be past that part of my life. But, now I was being told that was not true.

However, as Miss T said, that was how I was brought up and I was use to being punished for any disobedience, so I guess that was still better then living in the dorm and having to get a real job. Besides, all I had to do was obey everyone and I could avoid being punished anyway.

From my experience growing up, I did learn that I could avoid being punished by being obedient and I was very good at being obedient. So, that did not seem like a deal breaker for me as I thought how much trouble could I get into cleaning the house and obeying the girls and Miss T, or should I say the B.I.T.C.H.S.

Miss T continued to say that my attitude needed to be always polite no matter what happened or what someone said. Miss T told me that I was not to talk to anyone with permission unless I was responding to a direct question. In other words missy, you are here to serve us, not to live with us.

You are not part of the group of us 7 girls so you need to go about your duties quietly and not try to interject yourself into our business, even if we are talking about you. Understand? Yes Miss T.

Missy, Miss T continued; when responding to a question or order, you may just respond as yes Miss. You only need to use the initial when addressing the lady, as in excuse me

Miss T, may I ask a question? Understand missy? Yes Miss.

I was thinking the Miss T was turning this maid job into a real formal affair, but so far I had not heard anything that I thought was unfair or anything that I could not deal with.

Again, it still sounded better to me than living in a small dorm room with a bunch of guys. Additionally, I also did not need to get a job to help pay for my living expenses, as being the maid to the girls was my job.

Alright missy, Miss T said, everything seems to be going very well so far, but this next requirement you may have a problem with as you may find it embarrassing and or humiliating.

However, it is an absolute requirement and if you cannot deal with it, you can leave now. In fact, missy, when I tell you about it I don't even want to hear anything out of your mouth other then, yes Miss.

Miss T continued; the requirement is the curtsey! Come over here missy and stand in front of the mirror next to me. Miss T was dressed in a short flared skirt just like I was wearing and I now realized that she dressed like that on purpose just for that curtsey lesson.

I obeyed Miss T. However, I did so out of an automatic response to her instruction. However, CURTSEY? What the hell? I was not sure about that part, but I was willing to try it out and see what I thought.

Missy, Miss T said, before we start on the curtsey lesson, I want to point out to you that I just gave you an instruction to come over to the mirror and you did not say, yes Miss; don't make me remind you again, next time you will be punished! Understand? Yes Miss.

As we both faced the mirror, Miss T told me or should I say Miss T told missy to stand up straight with her feet level with one another and then move her right foot back directly behind your left foot, like this, as miss T showed missy.

Now, at the same time bend your left knee and only allow the toes of your right foot to touch the ground. Missy tried to follow Miss T in her actions and did not have any problem doing so.

Now Miss T said, this time using just your finger tips and you thumb to hold the sides of your skirt and pull the skirt out to the sides in a fan type motion while you bend your knees while keeping your back straight.

Good missy, Miss T said, now do the legs and the skirt and hold you back straight and dip with both knees in this motion. Now bring yourself back up by rising using your knees and drop your skirt and that is the curtsey. Alright missy that is a good start, Miss T said; you will improve with a lot of practice.

Now missy, you will curtsey;

When someone gives you an instruction,

Whenever you greet anyone, as in Good morning Miss T, curtsey,

When you answer the front door,

Last missy, considering there are 7 of us, you may greet us when there is more than one of us together as LADIES and curtsey only once.

Alright missy, Miss T said, we are moving along very well tonight, but let me warn you about curtsying. The curtsey is for showing the ultimate sign of respect and anything other than a perfectly respectful curtsey is consider being a disobedient act.

Missy, I don't care if you are embarrassed or humiliated answering the door or curtseying in front of one of the girls boyfriends. You will curtsey correctly, or you will be punished. Any laughing, or poor posture, or slumped shoulders or lack of dip length will ruin you curtsey and you will be punished.

Let me remind you one more time, missy, if you forget to curtsey or refuse to curtsey in front of anyone for any reason you will be punished and most likely you will be punished in front of that person. Understand me missy? Yes miss.

Having said all that to you tonight, missy, I do not want you to start until after you have had some time to perfect you curtsey. So I want you to practice 50 times each morning and then again each night. When I am happy with your curtseys then you can start curtseying for everyone else. Yes Miss, curtsey.

Alright missy, there is one more thing I wanted to cover tonight, Miss T said. Miss T handed me a wig and I put it on. The wig was a short black wig with bangs and was very thick so it really took over missy's face, so to speak.

In other words, the hair was what someone would first notice when they looked at missy as opposed to her face, so it made missy look more feminine. Miss T told missy that the wig she had was fine for serving at a dinner or going out of the house somewhere, however, it was too long and the hair would be getting in missy's face all day when she was at home just doing house work.

There I go talking about missy like she is a different person from me. Although, I guess missy is a different person then I am, but she is also the same as I like both of us. However, for the sake of my story, for both me and missy, I will narrate as if missy was a different person to avoid confusion.

In other words I will be my normal male self and will tell the story. Missy will be my female version that Miss T is turning me into, so let's leave her as my female version, missy, so we don't get confused all the time as to who's who.

Moving on; Miss T took missy over to the bathroom and washed her face to get off all the makeup that my sister, Jill, put on me before I met Miss T. Miss T told me that I looked like a clown and that she would show me how to put makeup on so that I looked more a real girl.

Miss T then took missy over to her desk and put some lipstick on missy's lips. Miss T put on some brown eye shadow to match missy's eyes. Miss T then had missy spread some cream concealer to cover any whisker effect and also put some blush on her cheeks. There Miss T said, now stand up and let's look at the whole package in the mirror, yes Miss, curtsey.

Missy looked in the mirror and was just thrilled. I really like what I saw as I saw a girl for the first time and not a guy dressed in girl's clothes. I found that to be so exciting, as it fed my desire to wear girl's clothes. Miss T again used her hand to feel my erection, or should I say missy's erection and she smiled, but she did not say anything.

I assumed that Miss T kept feeling missy's penis because Miss T knew what I knew and that was that when I liked something, like cross dressing, my cock would become erect. So I guess Miss T was using that as measuring stick as to my real interests, as my cock would tell no lies.

Miss T then told missy that she wanted missy to clean her bathroom so she could judge missy's cleaning abilities. Yes miss, curtsey. Miss T laughed at missy's curtsey and told missy that it was a good try but she needed a lot of practice.

Missy cleaned Miss T's bathroom for her in about 20 minutes and Miss T told missy that she did a good job but that she likes things done a certain way and showed missy how to clean the toilet better.

Miss T said that she expected the grout to be cleaned better and showed missy how to do a better job. It took missy about another

15 minutes to clean everything the way Miss T wanted it.

Alright missy, Miss T said, I think we had a good start tonight. Do you have any questions missy? No Miss, curtsey. Again Miss T giggled at missy's attempt to curtsey properly.

Alright then missy, until Friday night, you are to do the following;

Missy you will practice your curtsey everyday at least 50 times twice a day and by Friday I will expect only perfect curtseys.

You will put your makeup on every day, together with you wig and will always be fully dressed at anytime you are in the main part of the house.

Missy, you will clean the entire house as I instruct as we go through the week and everything will be subject to my inspection.

Friday night, Miss T continued; we will work on ladylike movements, like walking, sitting, bending, and posture.

Miss T told missy that she could have the rest of the evening off, but missy was to meet her in the kitchen Monday morning after missy got back from registering for classes to begin her cleaning duties.

Missy, you are dismissed, Thank you Miss, curtsey.

After I had some time to think about all of this missy female stuff and curtseying and being obedient and still being subject to being punished, I guess I was wrong about getting away from my sister as here I am still obeying Jill and being subject to her punishing me whenever she thinks it is necessary.

Additionally, instead of having my Mom around to punish me if I misbehave, I have Miss T taking her place.

That was the second time I was wrong about getting away from either my Mom punishing me, my sister punishing me, or both of them punishing me. The first time I was wrong about that was when I thought that when I turned 18 that I would not be subject to their authority any longer. I was dead wrong then and apparently I was dead wrong this time too.

Otherwise, my life would consist of going to classes and playing some tennis and baseball. I guess I will have some time to date as well, but I don't have any money to take girls out, as I only have enough to get by. Besides, with all that cleaning I will

need to do; I will not have a lot of extra
time.

For some reason not having the money or
time to date did not seem to be bothering me
very much and I thought that was strange.

As far as missy goes, missy so far is
pretty happy about everything. Missy did
not mind being the maid to the girls and in
a way actually looked forward to it. Missy
does not even object to that curtsey stuff,
it actually seemed natural to her.

Missy was also very happy about the wig
and the makeup and the fact that she looked
like a real girl in the mirror. That sort of
completed my long time interest in wearing
girl's clothes as now missy looked like a
real girl in the mirror.

Missy had the body for looking like a girl
as I am not very big to begin with. I am
only 5"9" tall and only weigh 137 pounds. In
those 5 inch heels I have very nice looking
legs, even better than two or three of the
girls in that house, especially Sandy and
Ida.

I had a great ass which looked delicious
in my short skirt and otherwise I had very
little body hair so shaving was really easy
for me. Even my face had a thin and slow
growing beard so it is easy for me to shave

very close and cover any shadow with only a little bit of makeup.

Time will tell how things turn out, but so far, both missy and I are happy with the arrangement. Missy even liked Miss T. Missy thought although Miss T seems to expect a lot, missy will learn a lot from her as well.

COLLEGE CLASSES:

The first thing I had to do Monday morning was go to school and register for my classes. I got there early so I did not have to stand in line very long, I hated standing in line.

I am not a big fan of standing in the corner either, but I could not avoid that when I was punished in the past. At least I am past that childhood punishment stuff like standing in the corner.

Anyway, I gave my class schedule a lot of thought. With my maid duties and the requirement to wear makeup I knew if I needed to go to a class I would need to take off the makeup and then reapply it again when I got home. I figured that would be a time consuming problem. Of course, that would have been in addition to having to change in and out of my maids clothes.

I solved that problem by taking all of my classes on Monday, Wednesday, and Friday's.

I had one class on Mondays, Wednesdays, and Fridays, at 10 am, another at 11:30 am, and the third at 1 pm. That way I was finished three classes by 2 pm. The 4th class I took on Mondays from 4:30 pm to 7:30 pm and the 5th class on Wednesdays from 4:30 pm to 7:30 pm. I would be home on Mondays and Wednesdays by 8 pm and on Fridays I was finished by 2 pm.

That gave me enough time to do anything I needed to do outside the house and I still had time to do homework, write papers, or study during the off hours. Even on Mondays and Wednesdays I had between 2 and 4:30 pm open for lunch and miscellaneous stuff.

I figured that I would not need more time than that because I always got good marks in school and never needed to study much. I seemed to be able learn and understand things very quickly.

That would also give me all day Tuesday, Thursday, and Saturday to do the house work without worrying about getting dressed and undressed and putting makeup on or taking makeup off. I could just live as a student three days a week and live a different life as maid missy on three days each week.

That left Sunday as a swing day to relax, play tennis or baseball, study, write papers, or even catch up on any maid duties that I had not gotten to everything during the week.

MONDAY CLEANING DUTIES:

My theory about getting to college to register for classes early very well for me as I was all registered and back home by 10 Am. Missy changed into her maids clothes and met Miss T in the kitchen about 10:30 am.

Miss T told missy that the house is really dirty as it has been unoccupied all summer and the kids that rented last year were not very clean. Accordingly, missy needed to work all week, every day, until she got the house up to decent standards for the start of classes next week, understand? Yes Miss.

Good missy, I want you to start here in the kitchen. Miss T told missy to empty all the cabinets and draws and clean the inside of each draw and each cabinet until Miss T was satisfied.

Then, missy had to put every dish, every piece of silverware, every bowl, etc thru the dishwasher before putting them back.

Additionally, missy was to clean all the jars or cans and everything else before it went back into its place.

While the dishwasher was working, which took three loads to clean everything, missy was to scrub the tile floor. Missy gave the floor a once over with the mop and soap that Miss T gave her but Miss T was not happy with the result and told missy that the floor was just too dirty to be cleaned with a mop.

Miss T told missy that she had to get down on her hands and knees and scrub the floor with a brush and Miss T gave missy some different cleaner to scrub the grout separately.

The dishwasher was finished its first load before missy was finished cleaning the floor to Miss T's satisfaction, which seemed to be taking all day. Missy took a break from being on her knees and restocked all the clean things back into the draws and cabinets. By then it was lunch time and some of the girls were coming into the kitchen to eat.

Miss T told missy that she could take a break and have lunch also, but Miss T reminded missy that she was to eat elsewhere away from the girls, either in her room or out on one of the unused patios and that missy was not to speak to them unless missy was spoken to first by one of the girls.

Missy said Yes Miss and went to get something to eat and took it to the back patio and ate their by herself, which was fine with missy as she enjoyed being by herself and she had no real reason to try to become friendly with all those girls anyway.

When the girls were finished lunch, Miss T had missy clean up behind them and put everything back into place either in a drawer or cabinet then finish cleaning the floor. By the time missy was finished just those tasks it was almost 3 pm and half the day was gone already.

Miss T told missy that in the future, now that she has the kitchen properly cleaned, that it will not take that much time and that it would only be necessary to clean the drawers and cabinets every 6 month or so, maybe more often if the girls tend to be dirtier then Miss T anticipate.

Miss T told missy that the girls, on an everyday basis, would be required to clean up after they eat to the point where they put all the dirty dishes in the sink and put everything else back into the cabinets or drawer. The dish washer was finished with the last load of dishes and missy put them all away.

Missy's normal kitchen duties would be clean the counters and table and put everything in the dishwasher and to put everything away. Missy also needed to vacuum the floor everyday with the mini vacuum in the closet.

Miss T did remind missy that she realized that missy's first job was to go to classes and study and get good marks and realized that sometimes those schedules may clash. However, Miss T expected missy to do the best that she could to be up to date on her cleaning.

Having said that it was time for missy to learn how to change all the beds and missy followed Miss T upstairs and Miss T showed missy that there was a closet under the stairway with all the sheets and bed spreads and cleaning products and pillow cases that she would need. The pillow cases and sheets and bedspreads were all color coded. There were two sets of sheets and pillow cases for each girl.

Miss T told missy that on the left side Jill would have blue, Beth would have beige, and Ida would have light yellow. On the right side of the hallway, Miss T herself with light purple, Miss Heather light brown, and Miss Sandy would have light green. Cathy had the room downstairs on the first floor and had all white.

The two large rooms in the back of the house went to Miss T and Jill. Beth's room was next to Jill's and then Ida had the room in the front of the house that shared the bathroom with Beth. Jill had her own very large bathroom as she had the bigger room with the private bath.

Missy was to make up all the beds that afternoon so everyone could go to sleep on clean sheets that night. Then missy would need to change everyone's bed one time each week, but not necessary on the same day, but as missy schedule allowed.

Missy needed to wash the pillow cases and the sheets while she cleaned the individual girl's clothes and put them back into the closets for the next change, along with that girl's clean clothes.

The bed spread needed to be taken to the laundry mat one time per month and missy should take three each time as they will be cleaned and dried on the same day so they can be put back on the same day.

Miss T showed missy how she wanted the beds made, which was very simple as the first sheet had elastic bands which hooked under the mattress so it fit tight. The second sheet had to be tucked under the mattress and folded over near the top of the bed and then the pillows would be placed on the sheets and the bedspread would lie over the pillows while tucked in under the pillows just a little.

Missy would be responsible on making the beds only on the days when she changes the sheets. The rest of the days the girls were expected to make a reasonable attempt to make their own beds as there just would not be enough time in missy's daily schedule to handle that everyday type of a service.

That effort took up the rest of the afternoon and it was dinner time already. Missy cleaned up after everyone had dinner and cleaned the counters and put everything in the dish washer and vacuumed the floor.

Missy went to find Miss T to see what else she needed to do that first day although missy was pretty tired already. Missy was not use to spending so many hours in one day working in five inch high heels.

Missy was hoping that her legs and ankles would get use to the high heels quickly. Miss T told missy that she was dismissed for the day and missy could go and practice her curtsying. Thank you Miss, curtsey, good night.

TUESDAY'S HOUSEWORK:

Tuesday morning Miss T had missy clean up the kitchen in the usual manner by making sure everything was in the dish washer and everything was back in the drawers and cabinets. Then missy had to clean the tables and counters and vacuum the floor.

Miss T told missy that today was bathroom day. Missy was told that she needed to clean 7 bathrooms that day. Miss T wanted them all cleaned the same way missy cleaned the kitchen with taking everything out of all of the drawers and cabinets and cleaning the inside of the drawers and cabinets and also cleaning everything that goes back into the drawers and cabinets before putting them back.

Missy was then to clean the toilets, bathtubs, or showers and the tile floors including all the grout the way Miss T showed missy. Missy then had to finish by cleaning all the counters and mirrors. Last missy needed to put all the new towels in

each bathroom that matched the color of
each ladies bed sheets.

The towels were to taken and replaced
with the clean ones in the closet every
time the sheets were washed, which was on
a weekly basis. Then after missy cleaned
those towels they become the clean ones in
the closet for the following week.

Cleaning the 7 bathrooms took an average
or 45 to 60 minutes each, so when missy
included time to eat lunch and dinner and to
clean up the kitchen after both lunch and
dinner missy did not finish until almost 8
pm.

Missy went to find Miss T and found her
in the office. Missy inquired if there was
anything else Miss T required that evening
and Miss T told missy that she was dismissed
for the evening, thank you Miss T, good
evening, curtsey.

WEDNESDAY'S HOUSEWORK:

Wednesday morning after breakfast and after cleaning the kitchen missy went and found Miss T who getting some exercise in the basement and inquired as to missy's chores for the day.

Miss T told missy to begin with going into all 7 bedrooms and taking everything out of each and every drawer and clean the inside of every drawer and then put everything back.

Missy knew what to do as this was the basically the same task as cleaning out all the kitchen drawers. Except that the bedroom drawers were just clothes and miscellaneous stuff, so there was nothing to clean except the inside of the drawers themselves.

Each of the smaller rooms had two bureaus of eight drawers each, or 16 drawers in each of those five rooms, or 80 drawers in total. The larger rooms had three bureaus with eight drawers each or 24 more times two. Then there were eight more drawers in missy's room. So missy had to empty, clean, and reload 136 drawers in total for the day.

When missy started in the first room she noticed that there was basically nothing in the drawers as the girls apparently were told not to unpack until the drawers were cleaned. Good advanced thinking missy thought, why put your clean clothes in dirty drawers?

It took missy about 3 minutes to clean each drawer so that took up almost 7 hours. Add in the time for having lunch and dinner, taking a break to get a few drinks and cleaning the kitchen two more times after the girls had lunch and dinner and again it was almost 9 o'clock at night already. Miss T once again dismissed missy, thank you Miss, good night, curtsey.

So far, missy's first three days were very busy. If I thought that missy had to work that hard every week I may have decided to go and live in a dorm with the guys.

However, I understood that once missy finished getting the house up to standards that it should be much easier to handle after that. So, one very busy week seemed like it would be alright with me and missy.

Additionally, all the girls seems very nice, especially Miss T who was very soft spoken but direct. Miss T conveyed the unspoken message to me that she was to be obeyed, PEROID! But, she conveyed that message in a very lady like manner that I found very appealing which caused missy to feel like she wanted to obey Miss T's every word.

SPANKING:

Thursday morning after breakfast, Miss T told missy that after missy cleaned the kitchen Miss T wanted her to clean all the windows in the house, both inside and outside.

Miss T also told missy that before she cleans the windows missy needed to take down all the drapes on the first floor and take them to the dry cleaners.

Then missy could clean all the windows. The drapes would not be ready until Saturday morning, so missy was to pick them up on Saturday morning and reinstall them on Saturday afternoon.

Missy hesitate for a minute and then said to Miss T, with an attitude that was challenging, OH COME ON, you can't expect me to go out of the house dressed like this?

Miss T just looked at missy and then said; well, missy that only took three days. Miss T pointed to a corner in the dining

area of the kitchen and told missy to go
and stand in the corner until she told her
otherwise. Missy looked at Miss T and said;
yes Miss, curtseyed and went and stood in
the corner.

While missy was standing in the corner I
was thinking that I had thought that standing
in the corner was not part of my future. I
had thought that I had stood in the corner
for the last time when my Mom introduced me
to the cane a few months ago.

However, as I keep seem to be finding out;
what I think does not matter very much. In
fact, what I think does not seem to matter
at all. The only thing that seems to ring
true was my Mom's advice to me; which was,
always obey the women in my life.

Anyway, about ten minutes later Miss T
came back into the room with all the other
girls. Missy became so extra embarrassed as
she was standing in the corner like a little
kid and all the other girls were looking at
her.

Of course, missy could not see them
looking at her as missy was facing the
corner. However, missy could feel their eyes
burning a hole in her back.

Miss T told the girls that it only took
three days for missy to disobey her and she

thought that maybe they wanted to vote on my punishment.

Miss T told the girls, or the B.I.T.C.H.S., that they could send missy to a male friend of hers he would give missy a good hard strapping. Or, Miss T could just give her an old fashion hairbrush spanking right there in front of everybody.

Beth spoke right up and told Miss T that she wanted missy spanked with a hairbrush right there in front of everybody. All the other girls agreed and that was that. My sister, Jill spoke up and said the she would go and get the spanking brush.

My sister also said that she would be happy to do the spanking unless someone else wanted to spank missy instead. however, Jill noted that she was happy either way, as missy could hear Jill leave the room.

When Jill came back with the hairbrush, Miss T told her that she wanted to spank missy. Jill handed the spanking brush to Miss T. Miss T got up and moved a chair away from the table and called missy over to her side.

Miss T sat down on the chair with the brush in her hand and told missy to turn around. Missy turned around as she could feel the intense heat in her face from her extreme embarrassment standing there about to get her panties lowered to be spanked right there in front of all the girls.

I have been spanked by my mother before in front of other people and even got that strapping that one day by that store owner. I found everyone one of those experiences extremely humiliating. However, now that I was 18 years old and in college and was about to be spanked in front of 4 new girls by a new girl, my face was so hot with embarrassment.

To make things worse for missy, Miss T told missy to go over and ask Miss Jill to lower her panties for her spanking. Missy knew that Miss T was only making her do that to humiliate her all the more in front of all the girls and it was working. It was working very well, especially since Jill was my sister.

Missy had no choice and missy knew it. Missy obeyed Miss T and turned around and while looking at the floor, she whispered to Miss Jill, would you please lower my panties for my spanking, Miss?

No! No! Miss T said, that's not good enough missy and unless you want to be punished for disobedience as well you will get it right the second time.

NOW! missy, you are to stand up straight, hold you head up high, look at Miss Jill and asked her loud enough for everyone to hear you! Understand missy? Yes Miss, as missy turned towards Miss T and curtseyed.

Missy turned back towards Miss Jill and obeyed Miss T and said, Miss Jill would you please lower my panties for my spanking, curtsey. Miss Jill just smiled at missy, maybe being a little embarrassed herself as missy was her own brother that was curtseying to her.

Miss Jill put her hands up under missy's skirt along both sides of missy's legs and started to tug her panties down to her knees. However, Miss Jill noticed that there was some resistance. Jill certainly knew from experience that it was from missy's erection that missy always seemed to get when she was embarrassed and or about to be spanked.

So Miss Jill had to move her hands to the front of missy's panties and pull the waist band forward so that the panties would clear missy's straight up cock. Then Jill was able to lower missy's panties to just above her knees.

Thank you Miss Jill, missy said and curtseyed to her. I could not believe how much that curtsey embarrassed missy, it was really bad, much worse than I would have thought.

Missy turned back around to face Miss T. However, as missy stood there with her panties being held up only be her spread legs. Miss T, as well as the other girls could see that missy had an erection as without missy's panties to hold missy's cock in place, missy's cock was tenting the front of missy's skirt. Obviously that intensified missy's humiliation greatly.

To make thing worse for missy, Miss T. took her hand and put it up under missy's dress and felt missy's cock as she looked at missy and smiled. Miss T did not say anything rather she just felt missy's hard hot cock and then let go and pointed towards her lap with the hairbrush.

Yes Miss, curtsey and missy lay over Miss T's lovely thighs and assumed the proper position for a spanking. Missy could feel the pressure on her penis as it lay over Miss T's thigh. However, did you hear me? I just said "her penis" as in Missy's penis. That was the first time I actually thought about missy being a "her", or having a penis.

Anyway, Miss T did not say anymore, she just flipped up the back of missy's dress to her waist to expose missy's own very nice ass to all the girls. Miss T started spanking missy very hard, but somewhat slow.

Miss T made missy feel every spank to start off with, but nonetheless, the spanks

were really hurting missy. Missy started to
kick her legs and squirm and make her crying
and ouching noises as Miss T just kept on
spanking and spanking and spanking missy,
maybe 25 spanks so far.

Missy did not forget that she was being
spanked in front of the other girls and was
therefore trying not to cry in front of
everyone. Missy tried to take the spanking
like a big boy.

But, missy could not help herself in
humiliating herself even more by taking the
spanking like the big sissy she really was
by kicking her legs up and down and squirming
all over Miss T's lap.

Miss T did not take any breaks to scold
or anything, she just kept on spanking missy
very hard with no real pattern, the spanks
landed everywhere, on one cheek, on the
other cheek, across both cheeks, up high,
down low, just SPANK, SPANK, SPANK!!!

After about 50 spanks or so Miss T did
stop and missy was hoping that the spanking
had come to an end and that she got thru it
without crying.

Miss T asked missy, are you learning your
lesson missy? Yes Miss, missy chocked out
the best she could while trying to survive
the spanking and at the same time thinking

about the show she was providing for the other girls.

As soon as missy chocked out that yes Miss the spanking resumed, only then the spanks were coming faster and harder, hardly enough time for missy to gasp from one spank to the next spank to the next spank and the next spank.

Missy could not hold out any longer and burst into tears and missy was no longer was in any sort of control over her humiliation level which was so high that missy could feel even more heat in her face from her extreme embarrassment.

About 50 more spanks were delivered before Miss T stopped spanking missy. Missy hardly noticed as she was just hanging over Miss T's lap crying and not believing how humiliated she was.

Missy just hung over Miss T's lap having her spanked bare bottom on full display in front of 6 other girls that were her same age. As missy thought about that, it just made her cry harder and louder making the whole situation even worse.

Miss T allowed missy to continue breathing very hard and cry for another minute or so before telling missy to get up and return to the corner. Missy slowly dragged herself off Miss T's thighs, wobbled to stand up straight, then chocked out a thank you Miss, curtsey.

Missy just hobbled slowly over to the corner and did not worry about finding her panties that flew off before the 25th spank. Missy figured that she would not need her panties for a while anyway.

Missy was correct as when she got to the corner Miss T told missy to hold up the back of her skirt to show off her naughty bottom to everyone.

Missy turned around and faced Miss T and while still crying a little and with tears running down her face that smeared her makeup, missy said, Yes Miss and curtsied to Miss T.

While missy was standing in the corner still sniffling a little, although all the real crying had stopped, while holding up her skirt and showing off her painfully spanked ass cheeks to everyone, missy was thinking about that spanking and all the humiliation that came along with it.

The spanking itself was not so bad, missy thought. Both my Mom and my sister have spanked me harder and longer than Miss T just spanked missy.

So, Missy decided that the humiliation of being spanked like a little girl in front of the Six ladies made the spanking feel much worse than it really was.

The humiliation that missy felt that day was certainly worse than the humiliation she experienced when she was younger when my Mom or even my sister spanked me in front of other people.

Before missy could finish her thoughts she heard Miss Beth tell everyone that she really enjoyed missy's spanking, how about the rest of you girls, what do you think?

Miss T laughed and said she was soaking wet. Missy did not know at the time what Miss T meant, but learned in the future that Miss T meant that her pussy was soaking wet as giving missy that spanking and humiliating missy that way sexually excited Miss T.

Beth laughed a bit and said yea, me too!

My sister, Jill said that she does not get excited in that way, but still enjoyed it very much.

Sandy said that she had never seen anything like that before and she found it to be very entertaining and that she might even want to try spanking missy herself one day.

Beth spoke up again and said that she surly wanted to have the opportunity to spank missy one day.

The girls started to talk about their classes and missy was able to finish her thoughts on which humiliating times were worse. Missy certainly thought that this time was the worst and at first thought that maybe it was because it was now and the other times were long ago.

However, missy decided that this was the worst of all for a few reasons. First, and most importantly, because missy is 18 years old and for an 18 year old to have her panties taken down and spanked with a hairbrush is extremely humiliation all by itself.

Second, again mostly because of missy's age, to be shown off having an erection before the spanking as if missy's cock was saying, yes spank me please, I love it.

The third reason was missy's crying. The crying part also came back to missy's age also. It's not so humiliating for a 13 year old or 15 year old to cry. But, for an 18 year old to cry, that's great humiliation all by itself. In fact, that may have been the worst part of the whole thing, missy thought.

The fourth reason was because of the way missy was dressed. Even though missy liked being dressed that way, it brings on a certain air of humiliation all by itself. If I were a guy and being spanked as a guy then that part would not be a problem.

Just then, Heather spoke up and said, WOW! Look at missy's ass it is so black and blue. Miss T you gave her a good spanking! I bet she will not sit down comfortably for a week or more. Thank you Heather, Miss T said.

After 15 or 20 minutes later, missy heard Miss T call her. Missy turned around, yes Miss, curtsey and walked over to Miss T. Miss T told missy to get down on the knees, yes Miss, curtsey.

As missy got on her knees, Miss T turned around so her back was to missy. Miss T told missy to put missy's hands up under her skirt and lower her panties to her knees. Yes Miss and missy obeyed.

Now missy hold up my skirt and I want you to kiss my ass with very gentle kisses all over my ass cheeks. Missy was instantly erect again and as she had not had a chance to replace her own panties it was obvious to the other girls that missy had the erection again as missy's cock was pushing out the front of missy's skirt once more.

Regardless, missy was very happy to see Miss T's ass as she had a great ass and missy was happy to be kissing for her. Missy wanted to do a lot more with Miss T's ass, but kissing it was all she was told to do. Missy kissed all over Miss T's ass and loved every kiss. Miss T told missy to stop and missy was disappointed.

Miss T told missy to get up and put her panties back on and get back to work. Missy got up, yes Miss, curtsey and found her panties and put them on and was about to leave when Miss T asked missy if she was forgetting anything?

Missy turned around to all the girls and said, ladies I am sorry about my behavior and will try to behave better in the future, curtsey. Missy hesitated for a few seconds and then faced Miss T and said, Miss T, thank you for helping me improve my behavior by spanking me, curtsey. Missy started towards the door when Miss T told her to wait once more.

Miss T told missy that in addition to her spanking and corner time that she also needed to give each girl their own private corner time. Missy was told that she needed to visit each and every girl sometime over the next three days when it is convent for the girls and stand in the corner of each of their bedrooms for 15 minutes.

Alright missy, now that we have dealt with your disobedience, the answer to your question about going out of the house dressed as out maid is that I expect you to be obedient, period!

Additionally missy, any cleaning time that you lose while being punished needs to be made up by you working longer hours. You may want to keep that in mind in the future as some of my punishment methods can take up quite a bit of your time.

Now! Miss T said, take down the drapes and take them to the dry cleaners! Miss T did not yell or really raise her voice very much, but the message was delivered with a very no nonsense tone that commanded obedience. What Miss T got in return was a very respectful yes Miss, a respectful curtsey, and of course obedience that time.

Missy got the step stool and took down all the drapes on the first floor and folded them neatly on the floor. There were three sets of drapes in the front of the house; one set on each of the two large front windows and one set around the windows around the front door.

There were three sets along each large window along the two sides of the house and three sets in the back as well around each set of double French doors. To take all the drapes down and remove their respective rods and fold them all took almost two hours and then it was lunch time already.

THE DRY CLEANERS:

Missy had a quick lunch and cleaned the kitchen after all the girls finished eating and then missy had no more reasons to stall from going to the dry cleaners even though she really did not want to go.

Going out in public dressed as a sexy French maid was not something missy ever thought she would need to do and she already felt the embarrassment that she knew she would actually feel going it to the shop.

Nevertheless, missy knew she had no real choice as missy knew that she would just be punished more severely until she obeyed. Missy's only other choice was to leave the house altogether and go and live in the dorm. That was still not an option for missy as far as I was concerned.

Nevertheless, leaving the house was the last thing missy wanted to do at that point in time. Well, actually, I guess it was the second to last thing that missy wanted to do as going to live in the dorm would be the last thing missy wanted to do.

Besides up until that point missy liked Miss T and liked working for her. So, after missy finished bitching about the whole thing in her head, missy took the drapes out and put them in her car.

Missy went back upstairs and washed her face and re-applied her makeup as her face was just a mess from all that crying. Missy wanted to wash her face earlier before she went back to work, but as Miss T told her to get back to work she was afraid not to do exactly what Miss T told her and nothing else, at the time.

Missy was happy that none of the girls paid any attention to missy when her face was such a mess of dried tears and makeup as that would have just made her feel more humiliated. When missy was ready to go she hesitated for a moment and then went upstairs and grabbed her raincoat and took it with her.

The dry cleaner's was about 5 miles away so it did not take long for missy to get there. Missy got out of the car and made sure her dress was smoothed out. Missy opened the back door to get out the drapes. Then missy paused again, Missy grabbed her raincoat and put it on.

Missy thought that although she was a guy dressed like a girl, at least she did not need to be so obvious being dressed like a maid. Besides missy tried to rationalize that Miss T told her that she needed go to the shop dressed as the maid and she still was dressed like the maid.

However, Miss T did not say that she could not wear a coat. Yes, missy really knew that was not Miss T's intention, in fact, missy realized that Miss T wanted missy to be embarrassed for some reason.

Missy, on the other hand, did not want to be embarrassed by going out in public and into the shop dressed that way. So, missy thought that Miss T would not know, so it would be fine. Missy needed to take three trips into the shop before she got all the drapes inside.

Missy collected the ticket noting the drapes will be ready Saturday morning and missy walked back to the car, put her coat back in the back seat and drove back to the house.

When missy returned from the shop she got busy cleaning the windows. Missy cleaned all the interior windows first on the first floor and was thinking about going to the second floor because she was delaying having to go outside in her maid dress to clean the outside windows.

However, missy looked outside and realized that the house was very private and no one would really see her. So missy went outside and cleaned all the outside windows on the first floor. Missy could not reach any of the second floor windows on the second or third floor. Miss T knew that and told missy that she would hire a professional with a ladder for the second and third floor outside windows.

By the time Missy was finished with the outside windows on the first floor, the girls had all finished dinner so missy went and cleaned up the kitchen, missy did not eat herself but did go up stairs to finish the rest of the interior windows.

By the time missy was finished it was almost 9:30 pm and missy was really very tired, especially her legs and her ankles as she was wearing those 5 inch high heels all day, for the fourth day in a row.

In fact, one of the reasons it took missy all day to wash the windows was because of how slow she needed to move up and down the steep stool and how careful her foot placement needed to be while wearing those high heels.

Missy was way too tired that night to go and stand in anybody's corner so she waited until the next evening to begin her additional corner time.

STANDING IN THE CORNER:

Friday morning, after missy cleaned up the kitchen and dining area after breakfast Miss T told missy that she need to vacuum the entire house and clean all the mirrors.

Missy looked for any indication from Miss T that Miss T was angry with her about the way she spoke to Miss T so disrespectfully yesterday, but did not notice that Miss T was anything other than her usual self.

However, missy did ask Miss T for permission to speak. Yes miss? Miss T, I just wanted to say that I am real sorry about the way I spoke to you yesterday. You have been very nice to me and I should not have spoken to you that way.

Thank you missy, I am glad to hear you say that. However, I do not concern myself with such small matters in the beginning as I expect my maids to have a problem adjusting to some of my requirements as some of my requirements are very unusual and sometimes hard to adjust too.

Nevertheless, missy, as you go through the training period and you find out that you will be punished for every single incidence of disobedience or disrespect, you will learn to just do as you are told and we will get along fine.

The only question for you missy is how often and how severely you wish to be punished before you learn that you are better off simply obeying me. In the end, you will be very happy to obey me and obey all the other girls as well, you will see, missy.

Missy, thank you again for your polite apology, you can begin your housework now. Thank you Miss, curtsey.

As it was a very old house maybe as old as a hundred years old, it had nothing but old wood floors. The owner decided it was easier to install carpet throughout the house than it was to maintain the old wood floors in any reasonable manner.

Additionally, carpet with its thick padding was the only way of making the floor quieter from all the creaking that one gets with old wood floors and old wood floor beams.

So missy had to vacuum the basement which was about 1500 Square feet, the main floor without the bathroom and the kitchen, was about 1000 square feet. The 2nd floor was about 1500 square feet, and the 3rd floor where missy stayed which was only about 800 square feet as a result of the shape of the roof line.

Because of the size of the house and the steepness of the stairways, someone decided it was best to have a vacuum on each floor. That stopped missy from having the problem of carrying the vacuum up and down all those flights of stairs in her high heels.

Missy started in the basement and found the vacuum in the closet and vacuumed the basement in about 30 minutes. Vacuuming was nothing new to missy as when I was my Mom's maid at home, I vacuumed all the time. However, Missy realized that this house was a lot bigger and it was a lot work vacuuming in her five inch high heels.

First, missy had to take much smaller steps then she would if she were not wearing five inch heels. Second, as missy was not use to all the work while wearing the five inch high heels, missy's legs were feeling the stress after a long week. After all, that day was the fifth day in a row, all day.

Nevertheless, missy had so much more to do that day and it was still early in the morning. To give missy's legs a break before vacuuming the next floor, she cleaned all the mirrors in the basement.

Missy realized as she moved around that her ass cheeks hurt from her spanking the day before. However, that was something that missy was use to and expected. It was really no big deal unless missy sat down on a hard wood seat. However, missy did not think she would be doing very much sitting down.

There were a lot of mirrors down in the basement; in fact one wall was almost all mirrors. Missy thought that since that was the exercise room that people that exercised like mirrors. It took missy almost an hour just to clean all the mirrors in the basement and then she moved on to the living room.

Missy vacuumed the living room, the office and the hallway in about 15 minutes as they was pretty easy. There were not all that many mirrors on the main floor as there were just a few round ones on the walls of the living room, and two floor to ceiling types on the hallway. There was one in the office and then the bathroom had one wall mirrored and the wall behind the sink was also mirrored.

Missy moved up to the 3rd floor and cleaned her own area which had mirrors in the bathroom on two walls and had two long wide mirrors on the one wall between the two dormer windows. With the mirrors and the vacuuming time of another hour plus, it was lunch time and missy was hungry.

By the time missy had some lunch and again cleaned up the kitchen it was almost 2 pm. Missy went to work on the 2nd floor as she figured that would take the longest so she left it until after lunch.

Missy needed to vacuum the long hallway, all 6 bedrooms and clean the mirrors in all 6 bathrooms, the mirrors in the hallway, and the mirrors in the 6 bedrooms. It took missy about two hours or so to vacuum and then almost another two hours to clean all of the mirrors.

The last thing missy did was to vacuum the stairs. There were three sets of stairs, all carpeted, and all very wide. Missy needed to vacuum the stairs on her knees as she used a hose wand to vacuum each stair and the back of each stair.

That alone took another two hours and it was almost 8 pm already and missy has not had a dinner and had not spent any of her time standing in anybody's corner yet. It was going to be another late night for missy.

By the time missy put the vacuum away and went to wash her face and fix her makeup and have some dinner it was just past 8 pm and she had to clean the kitchen yet one more time that day.

So by about 9 pm missy was finally ready to take her sore feet and legs to someone's corner and stand there embarrassing herself as part of her continuing punishment for opening her mouth to Miss T about going out in public dressed as a maid.

Missy went to Ida's room as missy noticed that Ida went to her room earlier that the other girls. Miss Ida, missy said with a nice curtsey, would you like me to stand in your corner for you?

Missy was thinking about what to say for hours before, hoping she could think of a way of asking without humiliating herself too much. After much thought, all missy thought she could do is simply ask, so she did and just accepted all of the humiliation that came with the task.

Ida who showed no real interest in missy or her spanking or her corner time just said sure, pick any corner. Missy set an egg timer for 16 minutes and chose a corner and just stood there until the timer went off. Missy turned around to Ida and said good night Miss, gave Ida a nice curtsey, collected her timer and left.

Missy noticed that Beth was also in her room watching TV so she went there next. As soon as Beth saw missy, she gave missy a nice big smile and told her to come on in. Missy also asked Beth, with a curtsey, if it was a good time to stand in her corner for her and Beth said it sure was.

Beth told missy which corner to stand in and missy set the timer for 16 minutes and went over to the assigned corner and stood in the corner for Beth.

However, not to missy's surprise, Beth told missy, well just don't stand there, pull your panties down and hold up the back of your skirt so that I can see your spanked cheeks!

Come on missy, Beth sort of barked at missy, you know the way I like you to stand in the corner! Missy did as Beth told her which added the additional embarrassment of having to hold up her dress while showing off her spanked ass to Beth.

Beth was correct however, Beth has seen missy stand in the corner many times in the past and missy knows that Beth, as well as Jill, like her to stand in the corner with her panties resting above her knees while holding the back of her skirt up so they could enjoy looking at missy's well spanked ass. So, that demand was not new to missy and therefore, it was not as embarrassing as it would be with one of the new girls.

After all, missy and Beth were good friends in a way as they grew up together, so missy was use to Beth and for some reason found it to be somewhat exciting in a way to be spanked in front of Beth and having to stand in Beth's corner with her panties down and her skirt up for Beth's pleasure. Missy did not understand those feeling either, it was just the way she felt.

A few minutes later, while missy was still standing in the corner Beth turned the TV off. Then a few minutes after that missy could hear some moaning sounds from Beth that got louder and louder and then missy heard some grunting and then everything was quiet again.

About three minutes later Beth started again with the moaning sounds. Beth's moaning sounds got louder and louder again and there was some more grunting and then quiet, again.

Missy was not sure what was going on over there with Beth, but she assumed that Miss Beth was masturbating as she looked at missy's spanked ass as missy stood in the corner. Apparently Beth found that to be sexually exciting for some reason.

I could remember during the days of the "hairbrush era' at home when Jill would have her panties taken down by Mom and Jill was given a good hard hairbrush spanking on her bare ass. I was there to see every minute of it as my cock found that to be really exciting.

I never did understand why watching my sister get a spanking was exciting to my cock and I still don't. However, apparently, my spankings and my corner time were exciting to Beth in the same way. You would think that that may really bother me, but for some reason it did not. In fact, for some reason, I felt closer to Beth as a result.

The timer sounded when missy's 16 minutes were up. Missy dropped her skirt and pulled up her panties and said good night to Beth and then gave Beth a nice curtsey and was about to leave the room when Beth told missy to wait a minute. Beth told missy that she wanted missy to kiss her ass that same way she did for Tara, yes Miss, curtsey.

Beth walked over to missy and told her to get on her knees, yes Miss, curtsey. Missy dropped to her knees and Beth turned around so that her ass was right in front of missy's face.

Beth told missy to lower her panties for her and missy said yes Miss. Missy reached up under Beth's night dress and lowered Beth's panties to her knees and lifted up the back of her night dress.

Then missy, who was rock hard, started to kiss Beth's ass all over. Missy had no problem with that order as missy wanted to see Beth's ass for years and really liked what she was seeing and kissing, that was great missy thought.

Miss Beth allowed missy to kiss all over her ass cheeks for a few minutes before saying alright missy that's enough for now. Replace my panties for me missy, yes Miss. Missy pushed Beth's panties back up and was sorry to do so as she was really enjoying Beth's ass.

Nevertheless, missy stood up and said good night Miss, curtseyed to Beth and left to go to bed as she was really tired and punished and worked enough for one day and one night.

Missy thought about standing in the corner of one more girl that evening, but after missy looked at the clock in the hallway she again told herself that she had enough for on every long day as it was after 10 pm already and she was tired and her feet were so extra tired from all the work and all the standing in the corner she had to do.

As missy was walking back to her room, Miss T was coming up the stairs. Missy greeted Miss T with a curtsey and said good evening Miss and went upstairs to her room for the night.

MOM TOOK MISSY SHOPPING:

Saturday morning came along before Missy was ready for it as she woke up with sore ankles, sore feet, and sore legs from all the strain from the last five long days wearing 5 inch high heels all day. But what choice did missy really have except to get dressed and meet Miss T downstairs to get her instructions for the day.

It took missy her usual hour to shower, shave her entire body, put on her makeup, and get dressed and go down stairs. Missy checked to make sure that her maid dress was dry from her hand washing of it late last evening before she fell asleep.

After all missy only had the one maid outfit and had to wash it every night. Missy had some cereal and a banana in her own kitchen and headed downstairs to see Miss T.

Missy entered the kitchen looking for Miss T and found her there along with

three of the other girls including Miss
Beth and Miss Jill. Good morning ladies,
curtsey.

Miss Beth looked at missy and gave her a
big smile as Miss Beth's face turned all red.
Missy assumed that Miss Beth was somewhat
embarrassed by having missy kiss her ass
last night.

While at the same time Miss Beth enjoyed
it and wanted missy to do it again. Missy
also enjoyed kissing Miss Beth's very nice
plump ass and also wanted to do it again
real soon. Just that thought was enough to
make missy's cock hard.

Missy went over to Miss T and curtseyed
and asked how may I serve you today Miss,
curtsey? Miss T smiled as apparently she
enjoyed missy's attitude and missy's
submission and missy's apparent willingness
to please her.

Miss T told missy that today she needed
to take down all the drapes on the second
and third floors and take them to the dry
cleaners. At the same time she needed to
pick up all the main floor drapes and bring
them home and reinstall them.

Also missy, don't forget you will see me
in my room tonight at 6 pm to continue your
training, yes Miss, curtsey. Missy could
only see another long day of work and work

and more work in those 5 inch high heels that she was not use to ahead of her.

After all, after missy finished all the cleaning for the day, she has another training session with Miss T and then has four more corners to stand in that night. Remember, that night was the last night of the three days she had to complete the punishment.

You remember on Thursday night, missy was too tired to stand in the corner and figured she would wait until Friday night to start. But last night she only stood in two corners, so now she had four to go.

In hind sight, missy should have stood in two corners on Thursday night instead of saying that she was too tired as now she has even more to do today. Then, missy had four corners to stand in which was an entire hour at the end of a long day. Alright, missy thought, enough bitching to myself, move on, get over it.

Missy went up the second floor and took down all the drapes on one side of the house and then went down and cleaned the kitchen from the girl's breakfast. Missy then went back to the second floor and took down the drapes on the other side of the house.

Missy put all those drapes in the car and then went to the third floor and took all those drapes down as well. That part took well over three hours. It was a slow moving process while wearing 5 inch high heels and while moving the step stool to each side of each window and taking down the drape. Then, folding them on the floor and moving the step stool to the next drape, especially as missy had such sore legs to begin the day.

Missy stopped to get a snack and then needed to clean the kitchen as the girls were finished lunch already. Missy then put the rest of the drapes in the car and headed to the dry cleaners again to drop off these drapes and to pick up the drapes from the first floor.

As missy did the first time, she put her rain coat on before going into the shop. Missy exchanged the second set of drapes for the first set and drove back to the house.

However, on the way back to the house missy was thinking about how well the rain coat idea was doing in covering up her maid outfit. Missy was thinking that she could never go out in public dressed as a maid with her five inch heels and her apron and with her legs on full display as it would be way too embarrassing. So, she was happy she thought of the rain coat idea.

When missy got back to the house she grabbed a quick snack and cleaned up the kitchen and spent the rest of the afternoon putting all of the first floor drapes back up. Missy looked at the drapes and thought that they did indeed look much better now that they were cleaned.

By the time missy was finished it was 5:15 pm. Missy needed to get something to eat and clean the kitchen again and still needed to be in Miss T's room by 6 pm. Missy just had a banana and some grapes and a few pieces of cheese and cleaned the kitchen and got to Miss T's room just before 6 pm.

As you know, missy was scheduled for more training that Saturday night with Miss T. However, Mom called and came over to take missy shopping instead. So, Miss T told missy that she would see missy in the morning and they would continue missy's training then.

I had no clue as to why Mom would be taking me shopping. However, to my utter humiliation, Mom did not come to take me shopping at all. Mom came to take missy shopping.

That was the first time Mom saw me dressed completely as a girl, with a wig and makeup and a bra and with my fake boobs. Mom gave me a good look over and then shook her head in approval.

Mom told me to change into my other maid outfit. My other maid outfit was my

original maid outfit that was more like a
tennis outfit, only I wore it with the white
pinafore that made it look more like a maid
uniform.

Mom told missy that she could leave off
the pinafore. Missy was sure happy about
that as at least she just looked extra sexy
with her short flared skirt and five inch
heels, but did not look like a maid.

Nevertheless, missy had no real experience
out in public dressed as a girl. Missy was
really surprised to find that Mom would
expect her to go out of the house dressed as
a girl. However, Mom just acted like it was
nothing, just like it was part of a normal
Saturday evening of shopping.

As much as all of that was over taking
missy's thoughts, never once did missy think
about disobeying my Mom, or even objecting.
I guess I had been so well trained over my
life time by my Mom and my sister to obey
them and then to obey them some more, not
obeying did not enter my mind at that time.
Strange, don't you think?

Anyway, Mom drove me to a shop about 20
minutes from the house. It was a strange
shop, the kind of shop that I had never been
in before, an adult shop.

I was just amazed at all the stuff they
had in that shop. They had all kinds of

leather clothes and underwear and bondage equipment, and lacy things, and all sorts of whips and straps and spanking brushes and paddles, etc., etc.

I had no idea why Mom would take me to a place like that, but then she walked me over to a rack that had all sorts of maid dresses. There were called French maid dresses, but looked pretty much like what I was already wearing only a bit fancier.

Mom had me try on every French maid dress that they had in that store that would fit me. I was so embarrassed being in that store being dressed as a girl and trying on girls' clothes.

However, Mom sort of rushed me though the whole thing so fast that I had very little time to think about anything except to keep obeying Mom. I guess in the end that was a good thing as I did not get myself in any trouble by trying to think about my public status of myself.

I tried on 8 or 9 French maid uniforms all together before Mom chose 5 that she liked on me.

Then Mom took me over the underwear section and had me try on panties and bras. I could not believe it! I was never more humiliated in my life. Meanwhile, Mom just kept moving along and picking out things

for me to try on like she took her son out
in public everyday dressed as a girl.

Finally, Mom decided on 5 pair of panties
and 5 bras to go along with the 5 French
maid dresses that she picked out.

The five maid dresses were all satin, and
all of them were basic black and white but
different enough so people would know missy
was not wearing the same one every day.

One was all black with white lace around
the sleeves, the collar, and around the
hem. It was tight fitting on the top and
had a fluffy skirt and could be worn with
or without a petticoat.

The second one was also an everyday sissy
maid uniform but more of a lose fitting dress
that would look better with petticoats. It
had a high collar and covered missy's neck
and was also very short.

The third one was made with petticoats
that made the skirt part stick out to the
sides and that made missy's waist look that
much smaller and also had a high collar with
short sleeves.

The fourth one was a very nice expensive
formal dress with a full wide petticoat,
high collar, and long sleeves. It was mostly
black in the body and the fluffy skirt part,
but it had white sleeves and was also white

on the top to the bottom of missy's bra
area. It was missy's favorite one.

The fifth one was really different.
It was all black with no white anywhere
except of the apron that missy would tie
on herself. It was very tight from missy's
neck to missy's knees. Missy was going to
have move around much more careful when she
was moving around in that dress as she could
only take very small steps as the skirt part
was so tight.

For the dresses that were not high up on
the neck, missy was given a collar to cover
her Adams apple which had missy's name on
it, maid missy.

Next, it was over to the shoe department
for missy to try on more five inch high
heels. After missy tried on about 6 pair of
high heels, Mom chose three for missy.

The first was a white sandal with five
inch heels that had a buckle that wrapped
around missy's ankles with a thin strap and
buckled in front. The part that missy toes
went into was made with six small straps
extending from a center knot.

The second pair was also white and had
a high part that wrapped around missy's
ankles and were tied up high up on missy's
ankles with a long white shoe lace and had
a big bow in the front. The toe piece was a

piece of leather that went across the front of missy's foot where her toes stuck out the front.

The third pair was black and was pretty much just like the while ones noted about, except that the tie in the front was a very wide ribbon type tie instead of a shoe lace type. Missy's toes also stuck out the front of those shoes.

Mom took missy over to the stocking area and picked out different types of leg wear. Mom chose a few pair of short white lacy socks that a little girl may wear with her Mary Jane shoes.

Mom also picked out some knee high stockings of white. Last, Mom chose some black and white full length stockings that would cover all of missy's legs.

The last items that Mom looked at were fake boobs. Mom bought missy a pair of bigger boobs that made her even look like she had a much better figure. Especially, when the bigger boobs were combined with a petticoat which made missy look like she had more hips then she really had.

Mom then took missy over and bought her a wig with long flowing hair as opposed to the short wig missy was wearing. The long flowing wig was really nice missy thought as I went half way down her back and had locks that would flow over her shoulders in the front to cover much of her face and give her a real soft look.

In the end, all five of the French maid uniforms could be mixed and matched with either white 5 inch high heels and white stockings or black 5 inch high heels and black stockings.

Missy could also wear her short lacy socks and have bare legs for a third look or knee high socks for another look. All the dresses were worn with a white pinafore of different sizes. All and all especially if you use the change of wigs missy would not look like she was wearing the same uniform for about four weeks, considering missy only works three days a week.

Mom told missy that Miss T would tell missy when to put in the bigger ones, usually at night if someone was coming to the house and missy was wearing one of her more formal maid dresses.

Additionally, when missy was to out in public on occasion, Miss T may tell missy wear the bigger boobs with normal female clothes.

All that was a lot of missy and me to take in. But, Mom kept the evening moving at a fast pace so that I did not have much time to think and to only obey her. That part

worked out well and kept my humiliation to
a medium considering where I was and what
we were doing.

However, when we were leaving and Mom
was paying for everything, the cashier Lady
asked Mon if she needed a nice whip or big
thick strap to help keep her maid in line?

Mom looked at the lady and said; thank
you for asking but my maid is very well
behaved. A good long hairbrush spanking and
some corner time is all my maid needs to
remind her to behave.

WOW, could that have been more
humiliating?????????

That night, when I was laying in bed
thinking about all the stuff Mom had bought
for me, I got very excited and had a throbbing
hard on. Apparently I was looking forward
to wearing all of those nice clothes, after
all.

SISSY MAID PRACTICE:

I woke up Sunday morning and my feet and legs were saying thank God I had a day off as they had a long week in those five inch high heels. A week of six straight, 12 plus hour days of cleaning and trying to do so while getting use to walking around in five inch high heels.

However, because of last night's shopping trip instead of missy's training session, missy needed to get up and get dressed and put those high heels back on and go see Miss T at 10 am. Hopefully I will at least get the afternoon off.

When missy got down to the living room just before 10 am, Miss T was already there. Missy curtseyed to Miss T and said good morning Miss. Miss T told missy to come in and let's get started we have a lot to cover this morning.

Before we begin missy, I have a few things for you. Miss T told missy that she noticed

that when missy walks around that she takes
big steps and that was not very lady like so
today you will practice walking like a lady.
Miss T explained to missy that when she
wears high heels she needs to take smaller
lady like steps.

Alright missy, Miss T said; the first
thing we will work on today is walking.
The first element of a female walk is to
have proper posture, in summary form Miss T
showed missy how to walk with her head held
up high and her shoulders back.

Miss T told missy that she was standing
well, but she also needed to walk while
maintaining that posture. However, Miss t
told missy that she also could not be stiff
in her movement, rather she needed to be
relaxed like she loved walking that way and
was proud of it. Over time, Miss T added,
it would be become much more natural and
wearing the high heels will be a big help.

Miss T then explained about missy moving
her hips properly. Miss T said that if missy
would put one foot in front of the other and
point her toes inward just a bit then she
would have somewhat of a natural wiggle.
Additionally missy needed to remember to
take very small steps or she would defeat
the wiggle effect.

Miss T then had missy walk around her
room back and forth so she could get a

feel for how much more work she had to put into her new walk. Missy was apparently doing alright, although Miss T reminded her several times to take smaller steps.

Additionally, missy, you need to point your toes forward when your foot lands on the floor so that both the ball of your foot and the heal of the shoe hit the ground at the same time.

In other words missy, you don't want to hear the heal of your shoe hit the ground and then the smack of the ball of your shoe. They need to land together so the landing of the foot will be much quieter. As well, missy, it will give you a much sexier walk and make your legs look sexier from a front view as you walk towards someone.

Miss T had missy go out to the hallway and walk up and down the hallway for her and again kept reminding missy to take smaller steps and to point her toes inward and forward on the landing.

Alright, that's enough walking for now Miss T said. The next thing we want to work on is bending. I know, missy, that if you want to pick up something you would just bend over at the waist.

However, wearing a short dress like yours missy does not allow for such a movement.

You are never, missy, and I mean never, allowed to bend is any manner where someone could see your panties, and I mean NEVER!

Miss T showed missy how to bend her knees with her knees together and to stoop down if she needed to pick up something or needed to put something down.

Missy tried it a few times and Miss T said that was alright for now. However, missy was use to doing that as Beth and Jill use to make me do that all the time at home when I was the maid at home.

The next thing Miss T covered was sitting. Miss T noted that missy will not have the need to do too very much sitting while she was working, but that she still needed to learn how to sit properly.

Miss T showed missy two ways of sitting, one as missy sat down she needed to smooth her dress beneath her and then would need to swing her legs towards the side or to the back with her legs together and her feet together as well and keep that position with her hands folded on the lap in the middle of her lap.

The other way Miss T showed missy was to just keep her legs in front of her with her ankles crossed and her knees together and also fold her hands in her lap over the middle of her thighs.

Missy sat down and got up and sat down and up and down for Miss T until Miss T was satisfied that at least missy understood her instructions. Miss T told missy to follow her to the kitchen, yes Miss, curtsey, and missy and Miss T went down to the kitchen

Miss T had missy practice all the new things she learned. *After about 15 minutes of walking from the kitchen down the hallway and back several times, stooping up and down, up and down, over and over, back to the kitchen and starting over. The more missy practiced the more missy started to get better balance and improve.*

Once Miss T was satisfied that missy was improving and maintaining a good attitude Miss T told missy to go and stand in the corner, yes Miss, curtsey. After about 10 minutes of holding steady Miss T allowed missy a minute to get a drink of water before they went on to the next lesson.

Missy your next lesson is an introduction to something called the kiss of submission, have you ever heard of that? No Miss, curtsey. Alright missy, earlier in the kitchen I had you kiss my ass in front of the girls to show your obedience to me. However, that was only part of what you will be expected to do after today.

Missy, get down on your knees and sit back on your legs and put your hands on your

thighs. Now as I turn around I want you to reach up under my dress and pull my panties down to just above my knees.

Then missy, just as you did before you will kiss my ass cheeks with a few gentle kisses on each cheek, pretty much around the middle of each cheek. Even before missy got to the kissing of Miss T's fine ass missy had a rock hard erection from just lowering Miss T's panties and see her fine ass cheeks.

Missy started kissing Miss T's ass and was once again missy was really enjoying the feeling of being on her knees with her lips on Miss T's soft ass. After about a minute of nice gentle kisses, Miss T told missy that she needed to use her hands to gently spread Miss T's ass cheeks a little so missy would be able to kiss Miss T's anus with missy's lips just like missy was just kissing Miss T's ass cheeks.

Missy obeyed Miss T and put her face into Miss T's ass crack and kissed Miss T's ass hole. Good missy, Miss T said, now do it again and give it a few kisses this time. Again, missy obeyed Miss T.

Good missy, you learn very quickly and that pleases me. Now this time, start from the beginning. Pull my panties back up and then take them back down, kiss my ass cheeks a few times and then spread my cheeks and kiss my ass hole a few times.

Missy did as Miss T told her and in spite of feeling very strange having to put her tongue on Miss T's ass hole; missy did find the experience to be a lot of exciting fun.

Alright missy, now I want you to do the same things from the beginning without me telling you. Missy again replaced Miss T's panties and then lowered them again and gave Miss T's ass cheeks a few nice kisses. In fact, missy lingered so long kissing Miss T's ass, Miss T needed to tell missy to move on.

Missy again used her hands to spread Miss T's cheeks apart as she leaned forward to get her face between them and give Miss T's hole another few kisses and then a few more kisses. Missy was really having a good time and was disappointed when Miss T told her that was enough for now.

Alright missy, now pull my panties back up and then rise. As I turn around you give me a nice curtsey and a thank you for the privilege. Good missy, now you know how I like the kiss of submission to be done.

Others may like it done somewhat differently, but that's the way I like it. If anyone else tells you that they like it different, then you can adjust you method to please them, understand missy? Yes Miss, curtsey.

Miss T had missy curtsey several times for her and found that missy learned to curtsey very well and told missy that now she was required to say yes Miss to all the other girls and to curtsey to them as well.

Missy sort of started doing that already on her own as it just seemed so natural to curtsey to the girls after she said yes Miss to them. However, now it was a requirement, every time, every day.

Missy, Miss T warned, and I do mean every time, a missed curtsey is nothing but disobedience and you will be punished. Understand missy? Yes Miss, curtsey.

Missy, Miss T said; while we are on the subject of punishment, let me tell you something you should know and you should keep in mind. I really enjoyed spanking you. Missy, you have one of the nicest asses that I have ever had the opportunity to spank and that made me enjoy spanking you even more.

Additionally, missy, I really enjoyed having you stand in the corner and I really enjoy humiliating you as much as I could in the process.

So missy, I will look forward to punishing you again and again as harshly as I think I need to in order to gain your cooperation and obedience. I will watch for that opportunity every day.

However missy, I try to be completely fair. I do not have any intention of punishing you unless you deserve to be punished by your disobedience or failure to follow a rule, which is the same as disobedience to me. So, missy, you are more in control then I am as to when and if you get punished. Understand missy, yes Miss, curtsey.

Let's discuss the next steps, Miss T continued;

One; neither Jack nor missy has the right to masturbate or cum in any way without permission from your sister, Jill, or from me, or from one of the other girls.

Understand missy? Yes miss, curtsey. But, I started to say. NO MISSY NO BUT! That is my rule and you can give me the thrill of your obedience or missy you can give me the thrill of punishing you further, it is up to you, now do you understand missy? Yes Miss, curtsey.

Henceforth, while standing in the corner, you will have wrist cuffs on each wrist and you will attach them behind you back. Understand missy? Yes Miss, curtsey.

Henceforth, you will respond to every question with a yes Miss, No Miss, or address everyone just the same, not just me. Understand missy? Yes Miss, curtsey.

Henceforth, you will ask permission to do anything that I have not instructed you to do. Understand missy? Yes Miss, curtsey.

Alright missy, for next week I expect you to practice everything you have learned so far this week and be able to do everything perfectly for me, understand missy? Yes Miss, curtsey.

Alright missy, you are dismissed. Oh, wait a minute missy that reminds me of one other thing I wanted to cover. When somebody tells you that you are dismissed that means that you thank them, curtsey to them and leave right away. It does not mean that you hang around for anything else, just leave. Understand missy? Yes Miss, curtsey.

Alright missy just one more thing for today. Since your Mon took you out last night and you were not able to complete your corner time with the last four girls, you can have the afternoon off to rest a bit and then do your corner time tonight. Yes Miss, curtsey.

Good missy now you are dismissed, thank you and good morning Miss, as missy gave Miss T a nice curtsey and left.

As missy was walking up the stairs to her room she was thinking about how her sore feet and legs are not feeling any better after having to wear those five inch high

heels over another long morning and her day
was not over yet, but at least she had about
6 hours to rest before night time.

When missy got back to her room, she
was going to get undressed. However when
missy looked at herself in the mirror and
saw a sexy French maid, missy liked what
she saw and decided to stay dressed for
the afternoon. Missy just stayed in her
apartment and rested her feet and legs.

Around 8 pm, missy took a drink of water
went back down the hallway and saw Heather
was in her room. Missy asked Heather if it
was a good time for her to stand in her
corner. Heather showed no real interest but
told missy, yea sure, come on in. Heather
did not show any more enthusiasm for missy
standing in her corner then Ida did, which
was no interest at all.

Missy thought that was a good sign for
the future as the less people interested in
seeing missy humiliate herself by standing
in the corner like a little girl was simply
better for her.

Missy set her timer, hooked her new wrist
cuffs behind her back and for the next 16
minutes stood in the corner by the window.
When the timer went off missy unhooked her
wrist cuffs turned around to face Miss
Heather. Missy said good night to Miss
Heather, gave her a nice curtsey and left.

Heather had no reaction to missy and just did not seem to care.

Missy looked in Sandy's room and saw her inside. So, missy said excuse me Miss, may I stand in your corner for you now, curtsey. Sandy told missy that was fine, come on in. Missy asked Sandy if there was any particular corner she wanted missy to stand in and Sandy told missy to stand in the one she pointed to, which was by the bedroom door which was where Sandy could see missy the easiest while she laid in bed and watched TV.

Since Miss Sandy had a preference to what corner missy was to stand in, missy assumed that Sandy would be one of the girls that would expect missy to stand in her corner when missy was punished for something in the future.

So far, Miss Jill, Miss Beth, Miss T and now miss Sandy seemed to like to have missy stand in their corner. Meanwhile, Miss Ida and Miss Heather did not seem to care for missy to stand in their corners. So that only left Cathy. Before the night was over missy would find out about Cathy and her opinion of missy's continued corner standing punishment.

Missy set her timer for 16 minutes, hooked her wrist cuffs behind her back and stood

in the corner on the sore ankles and legs
for the 16 minutes waiting for the timer to
go off.

When the timer sounded, missy unhooked
her wrist cuffs and turned around to Miss
Sandy and said good night Miss, curtsey.
However, Miss Sandy did not seem to care
much about what missy was doing. Missy left
and went on to number three for the evening,
which was missy's sister, Jill.

Missy found Miss Jill in her room and said
good evening Miss, curtsey; may I stand in
your corner for you now? Missy found that
request to be so much more embarrassing as
it was to my sister, even though missy has
already spend more time in her life standing
in the corner for Jill then even for Mom.

Miss Jill pointed to the corner of choice
which was the same corner Miss Sandy picked
out, the one by the door. Missy set the
timer for 16 minutes and went over to the
corner, hooked her wrist cuffs together
again behind her and stood in the corner
for Miss Jill.

A few minutes later, however, Miss Jill
came over behind missy and put her fingers
up under missy's dress and lowered missy's
panties and then wrapped missy's dress up
under missy's wrist cuffs so Miss Jill could
see Missy's spanked ass cheeks.

Missy was not suppressed as missy knows Miss Jill likes her to stand in the corner in that position. 16 minutes later missy's time was up and Missy unhooked her wrist cuffs again, pulled up her panties, and dropped her skirt. Missy turned around and said good night to Miss Jill, curtsey.

Missy got a big smile from Miss Jill that told missy that Jill really enjoyed seeing missy stand in her corner. That was no surprise to missy as she knew that my sister, Jill, loved to see missy dressed as a maid and loved to see missy punished and loved to see missy stand in the corner.

However, Miss Jill did not masturbate like Miss Beth did while she watched missy stand in the corner. Well, not at least while missy was still there. Miss Jill may have done so after missy left, missy had no idea and was not really all that interested to find out.

Finally missy was at the end of her corner standing night of punishment as she only had Cathy to stand for. Missy went down to Cathy's room and knocked on the door frame and said good evening Miss Cathy, would now be a good time to stand in the corner for you, curtsey?

Cathy looked at missy and said, I don't care about that, so yes, pick any corner you want missy. That was good news missy thought

as that was one more girl that would not be
expecting missy to stand in her corner for
her.

Missy set the timer for 16 minutes and
stood there until the timer went off and
then un-hooked her wrist cuffs and turned
around and said good evening to Miss Sandy,
gave her a nice curtsey and moved on.

After standing in those corners that night
for an hour total on top of missy's tired
and sore legs, missy just wanted to go to
bed. However, something was telling missy
that she needed to go and check with Miss T
first and missy took her own advice and went
back down to Miss T's room.

Missy went down the hallway to Miss T's
room and said good evening Miss T, curtsey.
Missy told Miss T that she completed her
corner time for all 6 ladies and would Miss
T like anything else before missy went to
her room for the evening?

Miss T told missy that it was very nice
of missy to come and ask her that question
as missy was not required to do so.

However, Miss T told missy that she knew
missy was tired and that anything she wanted
could wait until missy was finished all
her housework on Tuesday evening, so good
night missy. Thank you Miss, good night,
curtsey.

MISS T'S FINE ASS:

Monday was the first day of classes so missy at least got to rest her legs and feet while I took over that day and got to walk around in sneakers.

Tuesday morning, I had to get up about 8 am in order to be dressed and be missy by 9 am. Missy learned that by the time she gets up and showers and shaves her face and legs and puts her wig and makeup on and then get dressed it takes about an hour.

It took missy about 45 minutes longer than it takes me to get ready to go out on days when missy did not work. Those are the days I do not dress as missy and stay myself all day, usually on Mondays, Wednesdays, Fridays, and Sundays.

However, that first week was the exception as there was so much to do before classes started, so missy just had to get thru that first week and then things should be easier.

Missy saw my sister Jill as she entered the kitchen and Jill asked missy if she was enjoying her training, practicing, and generally being missy. Yes Miss, curtsey with a big smile.

I did actually enjoy being missy, in spite of the hard work, that first week. From this point on, missy knew that the house was be in better shape and would be easier to care for.

Nevertheless, missy turned all sorts of red in her face as she was embarrassed to admit to my sister that I was enjoying being missy. But, the fact was, that I did.

Miss T told missy that day that she needed to learn do everyone's laundry. Miss T explained to missy that everyone would have three sets of laundry. The laundry that goes in the washer and dryer, clothes that get dry cleaned, and some that may need to be hand washed.

First, missy, you need to go to everyone's room and pick up all 7 dry cleaning bags and take them to the dry cleaners.

Second missy, when you get back from the dry cleaners you need to go to my room and pick up my two bags. You take them upstairs and you put all the washer and dryer stuff that is white in the washer and you wash the white things first.

While the washer is running you need to hand wash anything in the hand wash bag. Jill tells me you have had plenty of practice over the years washing panties and a few other hand washables, so that should not be a problem for you.

Then missy, you hang those things up to dry. Next you put the white wash in the dryer and the colored things in the washer and wash and dry at the same time.

The reason I'm am detailing this for you missy is twofold, one, you can only handle one girls clothes at a time as we do not want to ever get anything mixed up. So, missy, if you only take one set of clothes for one girl with you at a time so you cannot make a mistake.

The second reason is time as you need to do 8 different washes each week including your own. So it needs to be a smooth operation to get everyone done each week. Considering, missy, that you are only scheduled to work three days a week, you will need to handle the laundry of two or three girls each day.

Now missy, Miss T continued; when you pick up each girl's clothes bags, you will also take all their towels, sheets, pillow cases, wash cloths, and or anything else they may have and wash them all at the same time.

Missy was thinking that as she needed to go to the dry cleaners again. It was a good thing that she left her rain coat in the car. Miss T? Yes missy?

By the time missy picked up the 7 bags and drove to the dry cleaners and drove home, it was already past 10 am. Missy started to work on all the laundry. However, as missy had found out throughout the first week, having to work and walk in those 5 inch high heels and take smaller steps so she would walk and wiggle more like a real girl was taking missy much more time to get anything done.

It took the rest of the day and into the early evening before missy was finished cleaning the kitchen twice and had all 14 bags of clothes cleaned and returned to their proper rooms and to remake all the beds with clean sheets and pillow cases and restocked the towels in all of the bathrooms.

Missy got something to eat and cleaned the kitchen for the third time and reported to Miss T Room. Missy was not sure what Miss T wanted her for as missy thought that when Miss T spanked her and had her stand on the corner in front of all the girls in the kitchen that that was Miss T's time of missy standing in the corner.

Nevertheless, missy was assuming that she was wrong and Miss T wanted her to stand in her private corner to complete her punishment. Missy arrived at Miss T's door and said good evening Miss, curtsey. Would now be a good time for me to stand in your corner?

Miss T did not say anything, rather she just pointed to the corner of her choice, yes Miss, curtsey. Missy set the timer for 16 minutes and went and stood in Miss T's corner while Miss T watched TV.

The whole time missy stood in the corner that night her legs and feet were in great discomfort from not only needing to walk up and down and down and up the stairs all day taking laundry bags back and forth to the washer and dryer, but also needing to stand most of the day hand washing panties and loading and emptying the washer and dryers, all in those 5 inch high heels.

The timer finally went off 16 minutes later, but to missy it felt like an hour. Missy turned around to Miss T and just to make sure she was being polite to Miss T, instead of just saying good night, missy asked Miss T if there was anything else she could do for Miss T this evening, curtsey? Miss T again smiled at missy's submissiveness and said yes there is missy; come over here, yes Miss, curtsey.

Miss T got out of bed and came around to the other side of the bed and turned her back to missy and told missy to reach up under her dress and slid down her panties down, yes Miss, curtsey.

Missy dropped to her knees behind Miss T and slid Miss T's panties down. Missy assumed that Miss T wanted her to kiss Miss T's ass for her real nice like missy did earlier in the week. Missy had no problem with that order as she liked Miss T and Miss T's ass and was happy to kiss it for her.

In fact, since Miss T was telling missy what to do, I found it so much better than me trying to get a girl to let me kiss her ass for her. It was not like I was trying to get a girl to have sex with me so I was not so nervous. It felt good to missy to have a girl just to tell her what she wanted. Missy thought that was pretty easy that way.

Anyway, that time when missy got Miss T's panties down to her knees, Miss T told missy not to stop there, take them all the way off, yes Miss. Missy slid Miss T's panties down to her feet and Miss T stepped out of them.

Miss T then lay over the side of the bed and told missy to throw her dress up over her back and for missy to move up between her legs so missy can reach Miss T's ass with missy's tongue.

Miss T told missy to start licking her cheeks, bite them a little, suck on them

some, and lick up and down my crack. Yes
Miss, missy could not wait. Missy's head
just dove into two of the greatest looking
plump but firm ass cheeks she has ever
seen.

Which being honest here was about two
ass's altogether not including Miss T and
Miss Beth that missy just saw that week for
the first time. Nevertheless, missy thought
that Miss T had one great looking ass.

Missy's enthusiasm was getting the best
of her and Miss T had to tell missy to slow
down and enjoy each lick, each bit, and
each suck. Missy obeyed Miss T and enjoyed
it even more. More importantly, Miss T
started to enjoy it much more and started
to moan and wiggle her ass around as missy
worked Miss T's ass over with her mouth and
tongue.

Miss T told missy to lick up and down her
crack. Missy was to start by licking just
along the top of Miss T's cleft. As missy
licked up each time she was to lick a little
deeper, until missy had her tongue all the
way inside Miss T's crack.

However, Miss T told missy that she could
not use her hands to spread Miss T's ass
cheeks that missy had to use just her face
and push it down in there. Missy was only
allowed to use her hands to hold Miss T's
hips on the sides to hold Miss T steady.

Now missy, start licking my hole just the same up and down and up and down like you are licking milk from a bowl like a cat. Missy did as Miss T instructed and gave Miss T's ass hole a good licking. As I noted, that was all new to missy, however, she seemed to be having a good time.

Miss T then told missy to dart her tongue in and out and smash her tongue against Miss T's ass hole. Missy tongue licked Miss T's ass hole as well as missy could and licked Miss T's crack up and down and dove back in again. Miss T seemed to respond well to missy's efforts and was moaning and wiggling her ass in earnest while saying that's it missy, that's it missy.

Then just like that Miss T told missy to stop and missy thought her had done something wrong. Missy stopped and just sat there on her knees waiting for Miss T's next command.

Miss T told missy to get up and remove her panties, yes Miss and missy did while wondering if Miss T was really going to let missy fuck her, how silly missy was, she knew better, but she was hopeful.

Miss T told missy to masturbate on her ass but to make sure most of missy's cum gets in her crack area. Yes Miss and missy did. It took missy only a minute or so to cum all over Miss T's beautiful ass as missy was so excited just from licking Miss T's ass.

Miss T then told missy to use her finger and spread the cum down inside her crack from top to bottom and even push some into her ass hole. Missy had the feeling that Miss T was going to make missy lick all of her own cum back out of Miss T's crack and out of Miss T's ass hole and off Miss T's ass cheeks.

Missy felt both excited and embarrassed at the thought of licking her own cum. However, missy did not know what to expect as she had never tasted any cum before.

Miss T told missy to lick up all of her cum and don't miss a drop missy, understand missy? Yes Miss and missy went to work repeating all of her previous movements only this time missy received a tongue full after tongue full after tongue full of cum for her efforts.

Miss T seemed to love what missy was doing as missy just tried not to concentrate on the taste and thought about how much missy simply loved the pleasures of Miss T's ass. Although, missy was not having a problem with the taste of her own cum, missy did find it gooey.

First missy licked both Miss T's cheeks clean of her cum. Than missy worked up and

down Miss T's crack area again. Missy was
thinking at least that way when missy got to
Miss T's ass hole she would not be getting
cum all over the rest of her face.

After missy gave Miss T's cleft a good
long cleaning with many long tongue strokes
from the bottom of Miss T's fine ass crack
all the way to the top, missy finally missy
got Miss T's ass and ass crack all clean.

Missy was having a good time as missy
again dove her tongue into Miss T's crack
and down to Miss T's ass hole and licked and
sucked all the rest of the cum out. Miss T
loved all of that and missy was wondering
if it would make Miss T cum.

Miss T told missy to tongue fuck her and
now that Miss T's ass hole was lubricated
with cum missy found that her tongue would
slid inside a little. Missy darted her tongue
in and out and in and out of Miss T's ass
hole and Miss T just loved it and squirmed
all over the place, but she did not cum as
far as missy could tell.

Miss T told missy that she could stop
and that missy was dismissed. Missy stood
up, pulled her panties back up, yes Miss,
curtseyed and went back to her room for the
night.

THE DOOR BELL:

So far over for the first 10 days of service as the sissy maid to the B.I.T.C.H.S, the hardest thing for missy to adjust too was answering the front door. It may seem like a little thing, but missy seemed to be extra embarrassed opening the door not knowing who was on the other side.

For example, one day the doorbell rang and missy went to answer it and found a very tall young man on the other side and told him good afternoon, my name is maid missy, how may I help you, curtsey.

The young man said that he was there to pick up Heather. Of course Sir, please come in and have a set and I will get Miss Heather for you. While you are waiting, would you care for a cold drink? No, thank you he said. So, missy told him that she will go and get Miss Heather, curtseyed to him and left the room.

Missy went and got Heather and the two of them went out on a date. It was a very simple thing, however, to missy it was one more person who saw her as a sissy maid. Additionally, it was on more fellow that saw me as a sissy maid. I did not seem to be bothered so much with the girls in the house, but guys, that did seem like a problem for me being missy.

THE DRY CLEANERS,
MISSY'S IN TROUBLE:

I enjoyed my first two days of college and did not find the subject material to be anything that I could not handle. That did not surprise me as I never had any trouble getting great marks in school.

When I got home from college on Wednesday I just stayed in my room and rested as my legs which were still pretty tired and sore and tomorrow was another day of five inch heels and plenty of housework.

Odd, I thought, after spending just Monday and Wednesday dressed as I guy again, I sort of missed my girl clothes. Strange I thought!

Anyway, Thursday morning started out like any other working day. I needed to be up around 8 am to shower, shave, put on missy's makeup and get dressed in missy's uniform and become missy.

After a long 10 days of being mostly missy 14 hours a day, I really did not feel like being missy that Thursday. The two days I had off were not enough for my legs to feel totally better from wearing those five inch high heels for so many hours.

I was hoping that I would get use to them over time as I understood that I went from not wearing high heels to wearing five inch high heels every day for 8 day of 10 days for 14 hours per day.

So, I sure could have enjoyed another day or two off. But, a funny thing happened, after I finished getting dressed as missy, I looked into the mirror and saw sissy maid missy in the mirror and instantly I felt like being missy again and everything seemed alright. Then, just like that, I looked forward to having a nice missy day.

Missy had some breakfast in my room as missy does not eat with the girls. Missy then went down to the kitchen and cleaned the kitchen as the girls all went off the their classes.

Missy thought that it would be a nice change as now she will be alone in the house and could just do her chores and did not need to worry about anybody hanging around or getting in her way, or interrupting her.

Missy also thought that if no one come home for lunch on school days that she would not need to clean the kitchen three times those days. Rather, just after Breakfast and dinner, which would save her some time as well.

Missy, found a note on the counter from Miss T telling her to pick up the drapes and other dry cleaning first thing in the morning so that she had enough time to get all the drapes back up that day.

Missy headed right over to the dry cleaners and once again as missy got out of the car in the parking lot she put her rain coat back on and went in and got all of the drapes and the 7 bags of the girl's dry cleaning and headed back to the car.

Missy's poor little heart missed a beat when she got to the car and found Miss T leaning on her car door. Miss T looked at missy and simply said, put everything in the car, yes Miss.

When missy was finished she looked at Miss T and Miss T told missy to put her coat in the car as well, yes Miss, curtsey. Right there in the parking lot missy had to curtsey to Miss T. How embarrassed missy felt just thinking that someone may have seen her.

However, that was not missy's biggest problem of the day as missy assumed that

Miss T was not happy about her wearing the rain coat to cover herself. It was funny how one minute missy was so proud of herself thinking about wearing her raincoat to protect herself from a great amount of embarrassment inside the dry cleaners and now missy was wondering how stupid could she be?

MISSY! When I told you to go to the dry cleaners as you were dressed, do you think that I meant that you could cover you maid uniform with a long rain coat, did you really think that is what I meant?

Missy looked at the ground and answered No Miss, Curtsey. Again missy was worried about someone not only seeing her in her maid uniform but seeing her curtsey as well. Missy's face flushed red hot from being embarrassed.

Nevertheless, missy developed a raging erection as she stood there in that parking lot that day in public for anyone passing by to see. Missy had no idea that getting scolded by Miss T would create an erection on her, but it sure did.

Missy! Miss T asked, do you remember all of my rules, ALL TWO OF THEM? Yes Miss, curtsey. Tell me my rules, MISSY! Missy repeated the two rules, obey everyone and don't do anything you are not allowed to do without getting permission first.

*That's very good Miss T said with great
sarcasm. So MISSY, did you disobey me
when I told you to go to the dry cleaners
dressed in you maid uniform? Yes Miss,
curtsey.*

*Missy was losing her concern about anybody
seeing her as she felt that she was in
so much trouble with Miss T that someone
seeing her dressed like a French maid was
not so important any more. Nevertheless,
missy did not look around to see if anyone
was watching her.*

*I am happy you did not play stupid and
lie to me missy; that shows some promise,
Miss T said. Missy, Miss T continued; did
you also do something that you were not
given permission to do, as in wearing that
long rain coat to cover the uniform you were
to wear? yes miss, curtsey. Missy, were you
not also being sneaky about it as well? Yes
Miss, curtsey.*

*Miss T told missy she appreciates the
fact that even though missy has been very
naughty at least she did not try to lie her
way out of it by offering stupid reasons or
excuses. Miss T told missy to follow her
back in to the shop, yes Miss, curtsey.*

*I guess that was not turning out like
a normal missy day after all. Missy was
becoming even more nervous following Miss T
back into the shop.*

For the first time missy was out in public dressed as a sexy French maid, with a dress hem that was blowing up a bit in the wind and allowing other people to see her panties in the back. However, once again, missy did not look around to see if anybody was looking at her, rather she just assumed that anyone around would be looking.

Miss T lead missy back into the shop and missy was just very happy that no one else was there other than the shop keeper and Miss T.

Miss T went up to the counter and said, good morning my name is Tara, I noticed you name tag says Nancy, may I call you Nancy or would you prefer something more formal? Nancy is fine the lady said.

Good, thank you Nancy. Miss T went on to tell Nancy that she has approved credit under the name of Tara T. I go to the university and will be sending in 8 bags of clothes each week from all the girls that live with me. Good Nancy said; I appreciate your business.

Miss T then said; Nancy this one, as she pointed to missy, who is standing over to the side looking at the floor trying to get past the great shame she feels from disobeying me and the great embarrassment she feels standing here in a public shop dressed the way she is, is my maid, missy.

Nancy looked at missy and said nice to meet you missy as she sort of smiled and sort of laughed at her.

Missy, already knew things were going to get worse for her in that shop, that morning, but somehow found the courage tell Nancy that is was nice to meet you also Miss, curtsey.

Miss T went on to tell Nancy that missy would be the one taking care of all the dry cleaning needs so Nancy would be seeing her almost every week. Nancy again looked at missy and smiled and said, good I will look forward to seeing missy then.

Additionally, Miss T told Nancy that when missy comes into the shop she will being wearing a maid uniform like this one or one that is similar. Nancy said that was fine with her.

However, Miss T continued, missy was already supposed to come to your shop three times dressed like that and she disobeyed me and covered herself with a long rain coat. Nancy said she was aware of the rain coat and wondered why missy was wearing it as it was not raining.

Yes, Miss T told Nancy, that is the problem and missy will be punished for her disobedience. Punished Nancy Asked? Yes punished Miss T said.

Miss T asked Nancy, in her youth, did she ever have the misfortune to be punished with a big thick leather strap? Nancy smiled and said no, but that her three brothers had some unhappy times on the wrong end of her father's strap, so I know what you are talking about.

Well Nancy, for missy's poor behavior, missy here, is going to be introduced to a big thick strap tonight. I have a friend that is a big strong football player that is going to make missy one very sorry little maid. Miss T asked if Nancy would like to attend missy's punishment, but Nancy said thank you, but I think not.

Miss T gave Nancy a card and told the lady that if missy ever comes into her shop again either without her proper uniform on or by covering it with a coat to please call she and she will thank her with continued business from missy.

Nancy looked at missy again and smiled and told Miss T sure, no problem. Miss T turned around and told missy to follow her, yes Miss, curtsey, as missy thought that she would die of humiliation.

Oh Yes, Miss T said, I almost forgot and Miss T turned back towards the shop keeper. Miss T asked Nancy, did you just see how missy responds with a yes Miss, and a curtsey?

Nancy smiled at Tara and said yes, Tara, I did. Miss T told Nancy that when missy comes into her shop in the future that missy was required to curtsey to her also when she thanks you for your service.

Missy just could not believe that Miss T was humiliating missy like that out in public, but what could she to do? Miss T added, and I do not care how many people are in here at the time, she is to curtsey to you and thank you properly every time.

Sure thing, Nancy said. Miss T thanked Nancy for her understanding and told her to have a nice day. Miss T turned and looked at missy and missy also said to Nancy, thank you Miss, have a nice day as missy gave Nancy her first proper curtsey. Miss T left the shop and missy followed her back to the car.

When Miss T and missy got back to missy's car, Miss T told missy that as she told missy before; she enjoys punishing missy and she enjoys missy's obedience and good service as well.

So from my point of view, missy, I can't lose either way. So missy, if you obey and serve me well, then I am happy. So you are disobedient and test me then you will be punished and I will also be happy.

So missy, Miss T continued; you need to decide if you will be happier being obedient or disobedient. I believe that in the long run you will be happier obeying me. I believe that I can turn you into a very happy sissy maid.

However, regardless of everything else I have said so far, I am very disappointed in you today, MISSY! NOW! Missy, you go home, you have a lot of work to do, and you need to be in the basement at 6 pm to stand in the corner and await your strapping. I would think after you are punished tonight, missy, you may have a better attitude toward obedience, now go, yes Miss, Curtsey.

It was not until I was driving home that my erection went away. That erection that started when Miss T scolded me in the parking lot continued the whole time Miss T humiliated me to no end in the shop. As well, it was still throbbing when Miss T was telling me about how I was going be strapped that evening.

Finally, when I got home the erection was gone and was replaced by fear of my pending strapping. I unloaded the car and returned everyone's clothes to their rooms and then put all the drapes back up. That took up the rest of my day as before I realized how late it got, it was after 5 pm.

I thought about getting something to eat, but thought that based on my experiences with full tummies and spankings that I was better off with an empty stomach, so I just had some water.

However, I gave a lot of thought to my upcoming strapping throughout the day. At first, I was thinking that maybe it was not worth being the maid around there if I was going to be giving strapping's by big strong football players.

But, then I thought, it may still be better to get past this one strapping and still have a nice place like this house to live in. The thoughts of a dorm with a bunch of noisy guys did not sound like fun at all to me.

Then I thought that if I did go to a dorm that I would not be able to dress as a girl like I enjoy so much and which is actually required in this house.

Last, I started to feel bad that I disobeyed Miss T. I was thinking about what my Mom had taught me since I was a little boy. Always obey the women in my life and I will be much happier for it.

Then I was thinking that I got myself in trouble only because I was wanted to avoid being embarrassed at the dry cleaners. However, that may have all been in my head.

Perhaps if I obeyed Miss T and exposed my French maid self in the dry cleaners that it would not be a bad as I thought it would be. Who knows, I never tried it before. Maybe I was making a big deal out of nothing in my own head?

So, I decided to accept my strapping and try harder to obey Miss T and everyone else and just stay out of trouble.

I went to the kitchen just after 5 pm and Miss T was there. Miss T, curtsey, may I say something please? Miss T looked at me and thought for a few seconds and then told me that if I was going to try and talk about my strapping the answer was no.

Missy, there is no discussion as to any punishment. I decide on the punishments around here and there is no discussion. Understand missy? Yes Miss, that's not what I wanted to say.

Alight then missy, go ahead. Miss T, I just wanted to tell you that I am very sorry I disobeyed you and I will try harder to obey you and please you.

Missy, are you telling me this before your strapping because you think I will punish you less harshly? No Miss T, I am telling you that I am sorry now because I think it means more before I am punished.

After I am punished, I will be more sorry that I was punished.

Miss T looked me over pretty good for about 30 seconds or so and then said. Missy, I think you really mean that? Yes Miss, curtsey. Well then missy, I accept your apology and I appreciate your apology as well.

However, missy, once again, now that you have apologized to me in advance of your strapping, I am supposed to feel less energetic towards punishing you?

No Miss, I would never think that. You see Miss T. once my mother decided to punish me there was never anything that I could say or do that would change that, it was set in stone. My mother taught me that once I earned a punishment, I deserved it, and I was going to get it.

I was just telling you how I felt Miss. I never expected you to forgive or forget any part of my punishment that I freely earned. Miss T, if you were to do that, I would lose respect for you and your authority and we both know that.

Missy, that is very interesting. I happen to agree with you mother and based on my experience training obedient maids, I think, missy that overall, you will be much happier after you learn to obey me as you obeyed your mother.

Missy, I thank you for your thoughts. Thank you Miss, curtsey and off I went to finish a few more things before 6 pm.

I was thinking over the next hour about my pending strapping and my apology to Miss T. I was really happy I decided to apologize to Miss T as she seemed to take it very well. I felt like Miss T and I had a bonding moment that I thought was real special. It was a feeling that I never felt before, but rather a good feeling.

OH MY, A BIG THICK STRAP:

Missy went to stand in the corner of the basement just before 6 pm as Miss T told her to and she waited. Missy was the only one there at that time. Missy was thinking about what Miss T had said to her earlier about being happier after she learned to obey Miss T as I learned to obey my Mom.

That was the same thing my Mom told me all those years at home and in the end Mom was right, Mom was always right, even when I thought Mom was wrong, she turned out to be right.

Missy guessed that by now she may have stood in the corner for about 30 minutes and maybe more which certainly confirmed that Miss T was really disappointed with her. Missy understood that Miss T really had a right to be disappointed with missy as missy knew that she was sneaky and was not obeying Miss T. Missy just thought she was outsmarting Miss T. I guess not!

However, missy was thinking that she could not seem to bring herself to go out in public dressed like a sexy French maid. Missy's thoughts were interrupted as missy could hear some or all of the other girls gathering, apparently to witness her strapping.

I could still remember the only strapping I ever got. It was by that shop owner a little over three years ago when I stole that lighter. That was as real thick strap and was used by a big man and it hurt more than any other punishment I ever had before or after that day.

So missy had to assume that the strapping Miss T told her that she was getting that night was not going to be anything better and maybe worse than my strapping. All of a sudden missy heard Miss T speaking and the voice of a guy saying Ok, Ok.

Then missy heard some furniture being moved and the guy said Ok again. Then Miss T told missy to turn around, yes Miss, curtsey as missy turned around and became instantly more embarrassed having to curtsey in front of some guy.

The guy was a big guy too, maybe 6"4' and about 250 pounds with big bulging muscles on his arms. But, that part left missy's mind very quickly as she noticed that the guy had a very long and very thick and

very heavy looking strap in his hand. Missy
started to panic a bit thinking that that
strap was even bigger and thicker and that
shop keepers strap.

Miss T said; missy tell everyone why we
are here at this time, yes Miss, curtsey.
Missy told everyone that she was there to
be punished as when Miss T told her to take
the drapes to the laundry mat, that missy
was so embarrassed to go inside dressed in
her maid's clothes like she was told to do
by miss T, that she took a rain coat with
her and used it to cover how she was really
dressed.

The whole time missy was standing there in
front of everyone being embarrassed by Miss
T, missy could feel her penis getting bigger
and bigger. Missy still had no clue as to why
that kept happening when she was embarrassed
or humiliated by Miss T, especially with a
guy in the room that time.

Miss T asked missy if she had permission
to cover herself and missy said no Miss,
curtsey. So missy, Miss T continued; then
you were disobedient? Yes Miss, curtsey.
Missy, Miss T continued; tell everyone what
happens when you are disobedient.

I am to be punished Miss, curtsey. Every
time missy? Yes miss, every time, curtsey.
Any exceptions missy, no Miss, curtsey.
By this time, missy's penis was at full

engorgement making missy feel even more
humiliated as she knew when her panties
came down everyone will notice when her
cock tented her dress in the front.

But, even before that happened, Miss T
came over and put her hand up under missy's
skirt and felt missy's erection thru her
panties and looked at missy and just smiled
at missy.

Miss T seems to like testing missy in
that way and Miss T has always found a hard
cock when she has checked. Missy wondered
what Miss T knew that missy did not know
about when and maybe why her penis would get
hard when missy is embarrassed.

Miss T Then said; well, let's get this
licking started. Then Miss T turned to the
guy and told him that missy's all yours. The
guy told missy to move over in front of the
bench that he just moved to the middle of
the floor.

Missy was not sure how to respond to him
so she was real careful and said yes Sir,
curtsey. Boy! missy thought, that was really
humiliating having to curtsey to a guy.

For some reason, curtseying seemed alright
and maybe even natural for missy when she
curtseyed to a lady. But, missy did not feel
the same way when she curtseyed to that
fellow.

Missy, the guy pointed to the bench as he told missy to lay down, yes Sir, curtsey. The guy then took that big thick long strap and laid it over missy's back.

The bench was obviously made for discipline, it did not seem to be of much use for anything else as the top part, that part missy laid on was shaped with a big hump in the middle so when missy laid down, her hips were elevated making her ass stick up in the air abnormally.

The guy fastened leather wrist and ankle cuffs to missy's wrists and ankles. Then the guy fastened missy's leather wrist cuffs to the front of the bench so missy's arms were stretched out tight in front of her and down towards the floor. Then the guy fastened missy's ankle cuffs to the back end of the bench so missy's legs were stretched out tightly also, but downward.

Then the guy took a another thin strap and wrapped it around missy's waist and tightened missy's waist to the bench so the she could not move at all. The Result was that missy was well secured to the bench and missy's ass would be a good target for someone to use a strap on as they could hit straight down which was much easier that trying to use the strap with a sideways target, as if missy was leaning over the back of a chair, for example.

At that point missy noticed that her
erection had gone away. Missy thought that
that was odd as that never happened before
she actually felt the actual pain. Missy
thought that perhaps it was because a guy
was going to punish her and not a female,
but missy was not sure. Maybe it was because
missy was just so plain scared at that point,
to the point where she was actually shaking
a little.

Miss T picked up the strap and came around
to the front of missy and bent down on one
knee. Miss T used the strap and ran the
strap thru her fingers in front of missy's
face.

Miss T told missy that she was very
disappointed that missy disobeyed her. I am
going to have this guy strap you and I am
going to enjoy every lick, missy. Perhaps
then, missy, you will be o=more obedient
and not so sneaky. Miss T smiled at missy.

Missy's heart skipped a beat, but Miss
T continued; my friend will give you 36
licks, 18 on each side, one lick every 10
seconds or so. Now, missy, you cannot kick
or move out of the way bound as you are, so
the only rule pertains to your mouth, you
are not to scream!

You may moan, you may ouch, and you may
cry like a little girl all you want, missy,

but no screaming, no begging for my friend to stop, or complaining it hurts too much. It's suppose to hurt too much, that is the purpose of punishment, to encourage you to not to want another punishment.

If the punishment did not hurt too much it would not be that effective. Do you understand the strapping rules? Yes Miss T.

Missy was really shaking in fear, almost like she was outside freezing and was shivering to keep warm as missy was sure that Miss T's friend could most likely deliver a very punishing strapping.

Alright then, who wants to take missy's panties down? Beth jumped right up and said she would. That did not surprise missy as Beth always seems to be interested in any of missy's punishments. I think Beth would be happier if she could strap missy herself.

Anyway, Beth came over and flipped up the back of missy's dress up over her ass to be folded over on her waist. Then Beth used her finger tips to gently lower missy's panties to just above her knees. Then Beth took a few second to rub her hand over missy's nice plump ass cheeks and feel missy up a little.

Then missy heard Miss T give her friend his instructions. Miss T told her friend to

strap missy as hard as he could and if there
was any sign of him feeling sorry for missy
or taking it easy on missy, that he could
always take her place, do you understand?
The guy promptly responded, Yes Miss.

Now I was really scared too as that guy
was much more capable of strapping me hard,
really hard. Missy just thought for a second
that not only was she going to humiliate
herself again by crying in front of the
girls, that she is going to be crying in
front of some guy too and that seemed to be
much worse for some reason.

At that Miss T pulled over a chair and
sat down on missy's left side. From that
vantage point Miss T could see the side of
missy's face and the side of missy's ass.
Look at me Miss T instructed and as missy
turned her head to see Miss T.

Miss T told missy that she sat here so
that she could see her face throughout the
strapping so that Miss T could see how much
missy was suffering from the punishment. I
love it when we make you cry, Miss T told
missy just to humiliate her even more and
it sure worked, missy thought.

Miss T's statement did cause missy's
penis to begin stirring again, but before
missy could think about it too much her
attention to what sounded like a gunshot
shocked missy. The sound was immediately

followed by the pain in missy's ass as the first lick from the strap was delivered.

CRACK! CRACK! Missy understood right away why she was so tightly secured to the bench CRACK! Otherwise she would have been off the bench as that strap hurt way more than missy ever imagined it would.

The guy certainly was taking Miss T's warning to heart, as he was CRACK! trying to punish missy as hard as he could and that CRACK!, was only four and missy had enough. Missy could not believe how much she was suffering, CRACK!

The guy started near the top of missy's ass and CRACK! He was working his way down the one side, just like Miss T did the first time she spanked missy. One CRACK! about every 10 seconds, just enough time for the pain to really sink in, for missy to yelp and yelp and yelp some more, while missy struggled in futility to get away.

The sound was so loud that it almost hurt your ears, but all missy could feel was a total deep down pain in her ass cheeks. The guy apparently knew how to, CRACK!, have the strap hit the center of missy's ass cheeks and then wrap all the way around to the side so the strap, CRACK! Covered the entire top part of both cheeks and then snapped over to where the leg meets the cheek on the other side.

CRACK! Missy at first thought that 36 licks did not sound like that much as she was use to getting up to two hundred or more from the hairbrush, but Crack! That was only 9, CRACK! well make that 10.

Missy took a peak over to see Miss T. I'm not sure why missy did, but Miss T was just sitting there watching missy's expressions and just seeing the smile on Miss T's face from watching missy's punishment and enjoying missy's punishment made missy feel even more embarrassment.

CRACK! The guy was down near the bottom of missy's ass now and her entire cheeks are just one mass of pain, so deep down, not like a spanking which was more surface pain, CRACK!, The guy was just beating missy like nothing missy ever imagined.

The guy was, CRACK! CRACK! CRACK! CRACK!, on the other side now, missy is about half way through that nightmare, just yelping and trying to kick involuntarily, and now crying more loudly like never before, CRACK! The snot was running out of missy's nose onto the floor, missy was just a, CRACK! mess.

At that point, CRACK! God that one really hurt, all missy could do was nothing, suffer thru that punishment and, CRACK! hope missy could avoid another strapping like that one forever. CRACK!!!!!!! Every

10 seconds, CRACK! they get harder to take as CRACK!!!!!!!!! the licking continued.

CRACK!!!!!!!!! Missy has have never cried that hard in her whole life and neither have I. CRACK!!!!!!!!!! Missy does not think that she would walk very well for a week or so with the, CRACK!!! Deep down bruises that the licking would leave, CRACK!!!!!!!!!!!!!!!!!!!!! Then it ended.

Missy just slumped like a rag in her bounds on this bench. Even though the licking came to an end, missy's ass was still hurting like nothing she ever felt before; it felt so swollen and was pounding in pain. That was 6 of the worst minutes of missy's life, certainly the worst licking of my life.

Miss T left missy there to calm down and stop whimpering and crying. The guy unbuckled the cuffs that stopped missy from running away. Then he helped missy up and helped missy walked back to the corner to stand.

Missy was still crying pretty heavy and was still having trouble breathing from all the crying and the stuffy nose and was still unsteady on her feet, but she managed to hang in there.

The guy brought missy a few tissues and allowed missy to blow her nose so she could breathe again and then he hooked her wrist cuffs back behind her back.

As soon as missy was able to breathe a little better Miss T told missy to come back to the center of the room and to kneel down. Missy turned around and said yes Miss. Missy could not curtsey with her hands still bound behind her back.

Missy assumed that she was going to either kiss Miss T's ass again or even have to give Miss T the kiss of submission. Considering all the girls were still there and especially that guy was still there, missy's humiliation was getting real high again.

Missy should never try to anticipate what Miss T plans for her as she always seems to be wrong. Missy actually should have thought about what would have been the worst humiliation possible under the circumstances. Missy would be more likely to be correct then.

As missy knelt down in the middle of the room, the guy, not Miss T, came over to her and put his back to missy's face and dropped his pants and underwear and Miss T told missy to give him the kiss of submission.

Missy just could not believe it, giving the kiss of submission to a guy? Missy thought that she could not have been more humiliated then at that time in her life. Not only was Miss T telling her to stick her tongue in a guy's ass, but missy had to do it in front of everyone else.

Nevertheless, what else could missy do? The guy bent over a little in front of missy's face as he needed to, to use his hands to spread his ass cheeks a bit as missy's hands were still cuffed behind her back.

Missy did the best she could to concentrate on the job at hand, or should we say the job in her face. Missy tried to ignore her feelings of extreme humiliation. Missy knew that if she embarrassed Miss T by doing a poor job that she would only be punished further and would still have to kiss that guys ass hole anyway. So, missy thought, she may as well do it right the first time. Oddly however, missy thought, she wanted to please Miss T.

Missy put her face into the ass crack of the guy and kissed his ass hole. It did not smell the best as the guy was a little sweaty from strapping missy, but missy kissed him anyway. Missy gave him about 5 kisses and then missy pulled her face out of his ass and leaned back.

Missy looked over to Miss T and waited for a response. Miss T told the guy that he can go and wait for her in her room. Miss

T asked if anybody else would like a kiss. Beth jumped up and said that she would. Miss T told her to take her place and Beth almost ran over to stand in front of missy's face.

Beth moved into place and with her back to missy she lifted up her skirt and pulled her panties down and spread her ass cheeks a little and missy stuck her face right into Beth ass crack. Considering Beth owned one ass that missy was happy to have her face in, missy was happy about performing for Beth, even with everyone else watching.

Missy gave Beth same real nice kisses to her ass hole and licked her real nice and then pressed her tongue against Beth's ass hole so hard that Beth moved forward a bit. Missy kissed Beth's hole a little longer than the guys but Beth loved it.

Missy was not worried about any of the other girls seeing missy kiss Beth's ass real nice as missy was really enjoying herself. When missy was finished and Beth moved away, the humiliation factor started to return, especially when missy was remembering about having her face in a guy's ass.

Miss T told missy that she could get up and go back to the corner. Missy got up, turned to everyone to face everyone and with her makeup a mess as most of it was dripping down her face due to all of the tears; missy told the girls that she was sorry for being disobedient. Missy thought that she should thank the guy also, but apparently he had already left.

Miss T asked the girls if anyone wanted to add any personal corner time to missy's punishment and Miss Beth immediately spoke up and said that she would. Missy's sister, Jill also said yes. Alright, missy, Miss T said, you will report tomorrow evening to Miss Jill first for 15 minutes and then to Miss Beth for 15 minutes, yes Miss.

Missy returned to the corner. However, a few minutes later missy was startled by a hand touching her ass. Miss T came over to missy and ran her hand all over missy's well strapped cheeks and said; my, they are very hot and swollen.

Missy, Miss T whispered in missy's ear, do you feel that licking was a sufficient punishment? Yes Miss T. Miss T told missy that she was glad her friend did such a good job strapping her as now miss T feels better about missy disappointing her. Perhaps now missy, you will be able to obey me better? Yes Miss T.

Missy guessed that Miss T did not feel missy was already humiliated enough that night, having to stand in the corner for her, receiving a tremendous licking from that guy while whimpering and crying like a little girl in front of everyone.

Then, having to kiss that guys ass hole, then kiss Beth's ass hole, and then stand in the corner again with her strapped cheeks on display. No, Miss T also needed to verbally humiliate missy even more. Missy did not find a big surprise in that, as Miss T seemed to be excited by humiliating missy.

Miss T continued by asking if Missy found it more humiliating to have a guy punish her than if Miss T punished missy herself. Yes Miss. Miss T asked if missy found it more humiliating to have the guy see you here like this standing in the corner like a punished child? Yes, Miss.

With that Miss T left missy's side and missy remained standing in the corner for about another 20 minutes or so at which time Beth came up to missy and also rubbed her swollen and hot strapped ass cheeks.

Beth could not get an erection reaction from missy as missy was still hard from when Miss T rubbed missy's ass and verbally humiliating her a little earlier.

Beth told missy that she just loved watching her get that strapping and almost creamed her panties. At least missy knew what that means now. Beth also told missy that Miss T wanted to see missy in Miss T's room, yes Miss.

Beth un-hooked missy's wrist cuffs and missy pulled her panties back up and smoothed her dress and thanked Miss Beth, curtsey.

Miss Beth looked at missy and smiled and told missy that she loves watching missy curtsey to her and that she will expect that for the rest of her life. Missy had no idea as to what Miss Beth meant and just left the room to go and see what Miss T wanted.

LICK WHAT?

Missy's first stop was to her own room so that she could wash her face and fix her makeup. Missy could feel every step she took in her ass and not in a good way. Missy got to her room and the first thing she did was to pull her panties back down and look at her ass in the mirror.

WOW! Missy thought, that was one black and blue ass. Missy could see the welts caused by the strap and in some strange way, missy enjoyed what she saw. Missy, remembered back when I use to look at my ass in the mirror for many days following one of my spankings from my Mom or from my sister.

For some unknown reason to me, I enjoyed seeing my spanked ass cheeks in the mirror back then and would look every day until all the marks and the black and blue was all gone. Now, missy seems to be enjoying the same view. Although, missy, sure did not enjoy how those welts got all over her ass.

Missy headed back down to Miss T's room. As soon as missy walked in, missy saw Miss T on her tummy over the side of her bed with that guy standing between her legs fucking Miss T in the ass.

Apparently the guy was just finishing as he was pulling his cock out of Miss T's ass and he went into the bathroom. Miss T said good missy I am glad you are here. I wanted you get lick me clean, both inside and out. Yes Miss, curtsey.

Missy was not sure that she should be doing such things, but she obeyed Miss T as it seemed to be the safer choice. Missy also thought that she had already licked her own cum out of Miss T's ass. So that guys should not be much different.

So, missy got on her knees and crawled up between Miss T's thighs and could smell a strange odor, it was not a clean fresh scent like the other night when missy's learned how to eat Miss T's ass for her.

Regardless, missy was obedient and started licking the guys cum off the inside of Miss T's thighs as missy could see the cum running down Miss T's legs. Missy was not happy with the texture or the flavor of that guy's cum, but she thought that that did not matter at that point. Missy told herself that she was there to please Miss T and not to worry about herself.

However, missy also wondered what that task had to do with being a maid? Nevertheless, missy was not about to challenge Miss T as missy thought that she had been punished enough for one day. Besides, missy liked Miss T's ass as was happy to lick it for her. Missy just decided that she would need to get past the taste of that guy's cum.

Missy licked up all the cum off Miss T's legs and then started to lick all along Miss T's beautiful ass crack. Missy licked up the cum with each long lick from the bottom to the top of Miss T's ass crack. Missy then moved her tongue deeper with each lick until missy had all of the cum out of Miss T's ass crack as well.

Last, missy licked all around Miss T's ass hole and then licked inside Miss T's ass hole the best she could to scoop out all the cum she could.

Alright missy, Miss T said that was fine, now go and stand in my corner, yes Miss, and missy got up, curtseyed, and went to stand in Miss T's corner. Miss T then followed missy over to the corner and when missy was standing there Miss T put her hand up under missy's skirt to feel missy's cock. Once again Miss T found a hard cock. Miss T went into the bathroom and took a shower.

Miss T came back in about 10 minutes and sat down on a chair across from the corner where missy was standing in and told missy to turn around. Missy turned around and said yes Miss, curtsey.

Missy do you believe that you can be more obedient now? Miss T asked. Yes Miss, curtsey. Good missy, I'm glad to hear that. You are dismissed missy, thank you Miss, curtsey.

Missy's legs and feet were very tired from standing in the corner for about an hour so far that evening in addition to working all day and still had two more corners to stand in that evening.

Missy went upstairs to get a snack and rest a while before going to Miss Jill's and Miss Beth's room to stand in their corners to complete her punishment.

Missy got herself a snack and had some orange juicy and went back down to the kitchen and cleaned the kitchen for the last time that evening.

Missy went to Miss Jill's room and said good evening Miss Jill, would it be convenient for me to stand in your corner now. I mean can missy's life get anymore humiliating having to ask my own sister a question like that?

Miss Jill told missy to come on in, you know what to do. Missy did know what that meant. In Miss Jill's corner missy needed to lower her panties and hook the back of her dress up over her wrist cuffs so that missy's punished ass was on full display.

As missy stood in Jill's corner that evening missy was thinking about how her sister thinks nothing of having missy stand in her corner with her punished ass on display.

Missy remembered when they were younger, just two years ago, when Jill cried and cried and cried just knowing that I would get to see her get a spanking from Mom and then Jill needed to stand in the corner with her spanked ass on display. How come it was not alright for Jill to be humiliated, but it is a great idea to humiliate missy. I never did get that.

Anyway, missy sent the timer for 16 minutes, and waited in the corner until the timer went off. When the bell rang, missy unhooked her wrist cuffs, pulled her panties back up and turned around and said good night and curtseyed to Miss Jill and went down the hall to Miss Beth's room.

Missy knew that Miss Beth wanted missy to stand in her corner the same way as missy did for Miss Jill. So, without being told missy went directly to the corner, set the timer, lowered her panties again, hooked the back of her dress up under her cuffs so to leave her bare as on full display for Miss Beth.

Once again while missy was standing in Miss Beth's corner, she heard a lot of strange moaning sounds from Miss Beth as Miss Beth lay on her bed. The moaning would get louder and then stop and Miss Beth seemed to be out of breath.

Then it was quiet for a few minutes and then the moaning would begin anew until it got real loud and then Miss Beth seemed out of breath again and then it was quiet.

When missy's timer went off missy unhooked her wrist cuffs, lowered her dress, pulled her panties back up, and turned to say good night to Miss Beth.

However, when missy turned around she saw Miss Beth laying over the side of her bed completely naked in the position just like Miss T was when Miss T wanted missy to lick her ass for her.

Miss Beth told missy I want what you did for Miss T, yes Miss, curtsey. Missy went over behind Miss Beth and got down on her knees and move up between Miss Beth's legs and just looked at Miss Beth's ass.

Missy thought that Miss Beth had one great looking ass. Miss Beth's ass was not a muscular as Miss T's rather it as more square and plump. Missy loved Miss Beth's ass and started to kiss Miss Beth ass cheeks.

As missy did with Miss T the first time, missy started licking Miss Beth's cheeks, bit them a little, sucked on them some, and licked up and down Beth's cleft. Then missy's plunged her face into two of the greatest looking ass cheeks she has ever seen.

Missy then started and lick up and down Miss Beth's ass crack, missy licked just along the top of the crack. Then as missy licked up Miss Beth's ass crack each time, missy licked a little deeper each time also until missy had her tongue all the way inside Miss Beth's crack.

Missy started licking Miss Beth's ass hole just the same up and down and up and down like she was licking milk from a bowl like a cat. Missy then started to dart her tongue in and out and smashed her tongue against Miss Beth's ass hole.

Missy's tongue licked Miss Beth's ass hole as well as missy licked Miss T's ass hole and then missy licked Miss Beth's crack again up and down and dove back in again. Miss Beth seemed to be loving missy's efforts as she was moaning and wiggling her ass in earnest as missy's tongue would press against her hole and lick all around it.

That was great missy, just great, now move on to step number two. Missy was not sure

as to what step number two was but assumed
that Miss Beth wanted missy to masturbate
on her ass and then lick off missy's own cum
as missy did for Miss T the first time missy
licked Miss T's ass for her.

Missy got up, yes Miss, curtseyed and
removed her panties. As with Miss T the first
time, it took missy only a minute for missy
to cum all over Miss Beth's beautiful ass
as missy was so excited just from licking
Miss Beth's ass.

Missy to use her finger and spread the cum
down inside Miss Beth's ass crack from top
to bottom and even push some into Beth's ass
hole. Missy knew that time that she was going
to lick up all of her own cum out of Miss
Beth's crack and out of Miss Beth's ass hole
and off Miss Beth's ass cheeks as well.

For some reason, missy was actually
looking forward to it. Perhaps missy liked
the idea of eating Miss Beth's ass more than
she first thought.

Missy was looking forward to it in spite
of how embarrassed she was at the thought
of licking up her own cum. However, missy
thought that licking up her own cum was
better than licking up that other guys cum
out of and off Miss T's fine ass.

Missy licked up all of her cum and did
not miss a drop as missy went back to work

repeating all of her previous movements only that time missy received a tongue full after tongue full after tongue full of cum for her efforts. Missy licked both Miss Beth's cheeks clean of her cum.

Missy, than worked up and down the Miss Beth's ass crack area again. Finally after missy got Miss Beth's ass cheeks and ass crack all clean, missy again dove her tongue into Miss Beth's crack and down to Miss Beth's ass hole and licked and sucked all the rest of the cum out.

Missy was even able to tongue fuck Miss Beth's ass hole better that time as it was lubricated with cum. Missy found that her tongue would slid in so she darted her tongue in and out and in and out of Miss Beth's ass hole and Miss Beth just loved it as she squirmed all over the place.

Miss Beth told missy that she was dismissed and missy got up, said good night, curtseyed to Miss Beth and went to her room for the night.

Well missy thought, her night did not start out very well, but she sure enjoyed licking both Miss T's and Miss Beth's asses for them even with the cum that she had to lick out of Miss T's ass. Although missy did not enjoy the taste of her own cum, she also did not like the taste of the guys cum.

But, then missy thought that she would get use to it as missy needed to assume that the girls would want more ass service as they both seemed to have such a good time. Missy found that she had a good time as well and would look forward to a repeat pleasure as well.

MISSY HUMILIATION:

On Wednesday missy got to rest her feet and legs some as I had classes all day and spent the rest of the night in my room resting and just doing some reading.

Thursday was a quiet day as all the girls had classes throughout the day which left missy on her own not to be bothered while she got all her cleaning and laundry done for that day.

In the morning missy cleaned up the kitchen and dining area after the girls had their breakfast. Missy started the dish washer and looked around to see what needed the most attention. Missy, was not given a schedule, rather just a lengthy list of duties and it was up to her to get them all completed each week to avoid any punishment.

With seven girls laundry to care for in only three maid missy days per week, missy needed to get at least three girls handled each day as she also had her own to handle.

So, missy decided to try and get three handed each day on Tuesdays and Thursdays and to leave Saturday available for the last girl and her own clothes or for anything that she did not get to during the week.

So, missy took the three bedrooms on the left of the hallway and took all their clothes and sheets and pillow cases and towels, etc up to her room where the washer and dryer were.

Missy laid the clothes, etc, out in order and started the washer with the clothes of the first girl. Then missy would work on cleaning that girl's room while the washer was doing its job.

Then missy would transfer that girls clothes to the dryer and start the washer with the second girl's clothes. Meanwhile missy would go back down to that girls room and clean it.

Missy would go back and forth like that until all three girls had all their things cleaned and dried. Then missy would take all their things back to their rooms and make their beds, hang up their clothes, put the towels away, and vacuum their rooms.

That actually would take more than all morning and run missy into the early afternoon. Missy stopped for a quick lunch and then she needed to head to the dry cleaners to pick up and deliver that weeks clothes.

Driving to the dry cleaners was not something that missy was getting use to very quickly as every time she still felt very embarrassed. Missy was not sure if she was embarrassed as she thought that other people could tell that she was really not a girl or if she was embarrassed just being dressed as a sexy French maid. Most likely both were the real answer.

Missy assumed that if she was a real girl and dressed in a French maid's uniform that she would still be embarrassed as it is not the way she sees other girls dress.

That particular day, however, when missy showed up at the dry cleaners there was a man inside in front of missy in line. When the man finished his business and turned around and saw missy, he stopped dead in his tracts and look missy over very carefully and very obviously.

After a long pause, the man told missy that she is the prettiest maid that he has ever seen and gave him his card. He told missy that if she ever wanted to change employers to give him a call.

Missy was both complimented and embarrassed by the attention. Nevertheless, missy, as she turned all red from blushing, thanked *the gentlemen for his kind words and gave him a nice curtsey.*

The man left and missy looked up to the clerk, Nancy. Missy said good afternoon Miss and gave Nancy a nice curtsey as well. Nancy had a big smile on her face and told missy that she sure made that man happy.

Missy told Nancy that she guessed so and tried to go on with her business and get out of there. The less time missy spent out in public the better missy felt about it.

However, not so fast! Nancy, or should missy say Miss Nancy had other ideas as the store was empty except for missy and Miss Nancy.

Miss Nancy asked missy if she was punished with a strap as Tara said she would be. Yes Miss, missy replied as she looked at the floor in utter humiliation.

Miss Nancy smiled and told missy to show her. Yes Miss Nancy, as missy lowered her panties and turned around to show Miss Nancy her well welted ass cheeks. Miss Nancy told missy that Miss T's friend did a good job of punishing you; do you think you learned your lesson? Yes Miss, curtsey.

Alright missy, you may pull your panties back up and here are your clothes. Thank you Miss, curtsey. Well, that was certainly humiliating, but what was missy to do about it? Not cooperate with Miss Nancy and get punished again. Missy did not think so and just obeyed Miss Nancy and lived with her humiliation.

By the time missy got back to the house it was past 3 pm already and missy still had a lot of cleaning ahead of her.

By the time missy cleaned the three bathrooms in the basement and on the main floor and vacuumed the basement and the main floor it was dinner time and all the girls were home eating.

By the time missy cleaned the kitchen after the girls were finished their dinner and got the dishwasher running again and cleaned the living room, it was way past 8 pm and missy had another long 12 hour plus maid missy day and she was tired.

Missy went up to her own room for the evening and washed her own clothes and took a shower and fell right to sleep.

SISSY MAID TEST:

Apparently Miss T told all the girls about what missy had been taught about curtseying and saying yes Miss and walking and bending and sitting, etc and they were all suppose to watch for any mistakes and bring their reports to missy's next training session.

So, that Saturday mornings training session with Miss T was to be held in the living room and all the girls were to be there. That did not please missy as she found being trained by Miss T enjoyable but with everyone else there it would just be humiliating missy thought. Nevertheless, missy had no choice in the matter and showed up just before 9 am.

Missy said good morning ladies and gave them a nice curtsey. Missy had spent a lot of time practicing her curtsey in the mirror and thought she was doing a pretty good job.

Missy was ashamed to admit it to herself, but she actually enjoyed curtseying as it made her feel submissive and feminine. Both were traits that missy was discovering that she enjoyed in herself.

Missy also liked to looked at herself in the mirror and it seemed that the more missy looked at herself in the mirror the more she enjoyed being the sissy maid to the girls. Missy really liked that, "sissy maid in the mirror".

Miss T told missy to stand over to one side of the room where everyone could see her, yes Miss, curtsey.

Miss T went over the check list from the girls. The only real complaint was that missy was not keeping her knees together all the time when she was stooping down.

While all the girls sat around chatting, Missy served breakfast and drinks and practiced walking, curtsies, serving, and stooping. After about 30 minutes, Miss T told missy to go and stand in the corner, yes Miss, curtsey. Miss T had missy spend 15 minutes standing in the corner with proper posture.

Miss T asked the girls what they thought about missy performance over the past hour or so. Everyone was happy except Miss Jill who noted missy's continuing problem of not keeping her knees together when stooping.

Miss T said that she agreed and that she could not let that go any longer. Miss T noted that missy should have mastered that movement by now.

Alright, missy, Miss T said, I want you to stand in the corner there for another 30 minutes with your knees together. Then I will give you a different type of dress that will help you practice keeping your knees together when you stoop down.

Miss T asked the girls if anyone wanted additional private corner time from missy that evening. Miss Beth was the only one to say yes that time, so Miss T told missy to report to Miss Beth's room later that evening. Yes Miss, curtsey, as missy moved over to stand in the corner.

As missy was standing in the corner, the door bell rang. Miss T answered the door and introduced herself to a young man that came to see Miss Heather. Miss T invited him inside and told him to have a seat and she would tell Heather that he was here.

However, before Miss T left the room, she told the young man not to worry about missy. Missy is just a naughty maid that was being punished. Well, that was sure humiliating. I mean, suppose I meet that fellow on campus and he knows I am that maid; my secret would be out forever.

Missy also thought that it was a good thing that she was facing the corner as he could not see her face. Missy thought that was the only thing that saved her. But, then missy started to think about the future and wondered what would happen when guys started coming to the house when she was working and they could see her face.

That was not something missy ever thought about before as I just always assumed missy's maid life here would remain missy's maid life in the house. Now, I was worried and embarrassed in advance of the unknown.

Miss T called missy over to her when her corner time was over. Alright then missy, a couple of more things and you can get on with your cleaning.

First, we want you to wear black toe nail polish from now on.

Second, we want you to wear clear nail polish on your finger nails.

Third, as Miss T handed missy a new dress, she told missy to go and put the dress on and wear it for the rest of the day.

Missy took the dress and went back to her room to put on the toe nail and finger nail polish that Miss T gave her and to put on her new dress.

The dress, as missy learned later, was called a hobble dress. It was one of the dresses that Mom bought for missy last Saturday night when Mom took missy shopping. The dress was all black but it was much longer than any of missy's other dresses.

The dress came down to missy's knees and had strings to tie the skirt part real tight around missy's legs. Obviously, the purpose was so missy could not move her legs apart more than a few inches.

Missy tried to walk in the hobble dress and found that she could only take very small steps like Miss T wanted her to take anyway. However, missy also discovered that she could not bend over.

If missy was to lean forward the dress in the back would grab at her neck and she could not breathe. So missy realized that while wearing that dress she would need to stoop down for everything and anything and she had to keep her knees together as well.

Missy had no trouble getting use to walking and moving in the hobble dress, however missy did find out that it took much longer to get anything done as she was so restricted in her movements.

On the bright side, missy thought that her ass looked great in that dress as it *was so tight and wrapped around her ass real nice. Missy did figure that the dress would help her learn to keep her knees together and to stoop the way the girls wanted her too.*

Otherwise, missy did not like that dress compared to all her other short fluffy dresses.

HOME ALONE:

Later that day all the girls had gone out, so missy was home alone. Missy had just finished cleaning the kitchen and getting the dish washer going when the doorbell rang.

Missy really did not like answering the door, but she knew that she had too. Additionally, missy was instructed by Miss T as to how to answer the door in the most embarrassing way. So, missy opened the door and said; good morning Sir, my name is maid missy, how may I help you, curtsey.

Missy hated the requirement to curtsey to strangers at the door, but what could she do. The man at the door gave missy a huge smile and told missy that he was antenna man and he was called to come and adjust the TV antenna.

Missy asked him if he needed to come in the house or if he just needed to go on the roof. The man told missy both and asked to

see the nearest TV. Missy showed him the TV
in the living room.

He turned on the TV and looked at the
picture and then told missy that he would be
right back that now he needed to go on the
roof and move the antenna a little.

As missy watched the TV, the picture did
get better and then the man came back and
told missy that he was finished. He collected
his bag of tools and missy walked him to the
front door.

As he was leaving he told missy that she
was a very pretty maid and asked if she
had a boyfriend? Missy turned all shades
of red as she was totally embarrassed, yet
complemented at the same time.

Missy, smiled and told him that yes she
does have a boyfriend, but thank you anyway,
Sir, curtsey. Missy got another huge smile
from the young man and off he went.

Missy was thinking that she must really
look like a girl as that was the second guy
so far that month that wanted to either date
her or hire her.

THE CANE:

The following week went pretty smooth as I went to classes for my three days and missy worked her two days and there was not anything worth mentioning to you about that week.

However, on Saturday morning missy was just finished cleaning the kitchen and dining room and put everything away and started the dishwasher when Miss Ida came into the kitchen and made a mess again.

Missy, who had a lot to do that Saturday, sort of got upset with Miss Ida and complained to her about her poor timing. Ida just turned around and gave missy a mean face and told missy to go and ask Miss T to come to the kitchen as Ida kept eating. Yes Miss, curtsey.

Missy had to assume that she got herself in trouble again as missy would never have been permitted to speak to Miss T that way. In fact missy surly would not get away with speaking to Miss Jill or Miss Beth, with that type of a tone either.

Missy found Miss T in her bedroom and told Miss T what she had done and that Miss Ida would like her to come to the kitchen. Miss T looked at missy and said; did you really speak to Miss Ida that way. Missy dropped her head in shame and said yes Miss T, curtsey.

Alright missy, I am disappointed in you, but let's go and see what Miss Ida has to say about it before I decide on your punishment, yes Miss, curtsey. Missy, followed Miss T back to the kitchen and Miss Ida told Miss T the same story that missy told Miss T, almost word for word.

Well, missy, as Miss T looked over at missy, I have two things to say to you. First, there is no reason for you ever to be disrespectful to anyone. If you have a problem with someone, missy, you know you are to come to me, correct missy? Yes Miss, curtsey.

Second, and more important to me, missy. You told me the truth, the whole truth, and took reasonability for you mistake even thought you knew you would be punished. To me missy, that is more important and I need to tell you that I am ever so pleased with you and your attitude and the way you handled this matter.

Nevertheless, missy, we cannot have you opening your mouth to the ladies of this house, or anyone else for that matter. So, missy, I am going to introduce you to the CANE.

Alright missy, you go down to the basement and stand in the corner and we will take care of your punishment right now. Missy, I know you have a lot to do today and you just cost yourself an extra hour which you will need to make up tonight before you can go to bed, yes Miss, curtsey.

Missy went down to the basement and put her wrist cuffs on and hooked them behind her back and went and waited in the corner until Miss T came down to cane her.

Missy had never been caned before except that one time I was caned by Mom. So missy was unsure as to what to expect from Miss T. Obviously it was going to hurt, but how much missy was unsure of.

Nevertheless, missy was real nervous as she really did not want to find out how much the cane would hurt and she was also worried if all the girls would come and watch her get punished and cry again in front of them. Crying in front of the girls was the one thing that missy kept thinking about as it embarrassed her the most.

About 15 minutes later Miss T told missy to turn around. In addition to Miss T, Miss Ida, Miss Jill, and Miss Beth were there. Missy assumed that the other three girls did not care to see missy punished.

Miss T asked if any of the girls wanted to handle securing missy to the punishment bench and Miss Beth almost jumped off the couch to volunteer first. Miss T, sort of laughed at Miss Beth's enthusiasm, but told Beth to go ahead.

The punishment bench was still in the middle of the room from last time it was used by that guy who gave missy that strapping. Missy still had some faded welts on her ass cheeks from that strap.

Beth told missy to lay down, yes Miss, curtsey and missy laid down across the bench. Beth attached missy's wrist cuffs to the bottom of the bench's legs in the front. Beth put ankle cuffs on missy's ankles and attached them to the back legs of the bench. Then, Miss T handed Miss Beth a strap to put around missy's waist to hold her tight to the bench.

However, after Miss Beth affixed missy's waist to the bench, she moved over to missy's side and whispered to missy that she was going to cream her panties when missy started crying in earnest. WOW! that sure made missy feel a lot better, NOT!

As Miss Beth got back to the couch and took her set, Miss T called to Beth and asked her; what about missy's panties, Beth? OH! Beth jumped back up and came over and flipped up missy's dress up over her hips and then lowered missy's panties to rest around her knees. Thank you, Beth.

Beth took her seat again and the canning began. Missy could tell from the very first stroke that Miss T was going to teach her some lesson that morning. The first stroke stung like a hundred bees for about 10 seconds, and then the second stroke landed. Miss T continued caning missy's cheeks with hard whistling strokes of her cane in about 15 seconds intervals.

By only the fifth stroke missy started to moan and breath much more heavily. By the 10th stroke missy was almost crying and moaning in between strokes as all 10 welts seemed to hurt at the same time. Which of course was the idea of proceeding more slowly?

After Miss T delivered 25 strokes and gave missy 25 welts. Missy had had enough and was hurting pretty bad, squirming a lot more and crying in earnest at that point. The 25 welts took about 5 to 6 minutes to deliver at one every 15 seconds or so.

The cane give a lasting sting to missy after Miss T whistled it through the air and it struck across missy's nice ass cheeks. Then when the cane tip whipped around the side of missy's cheeks it really hurt a lot more as there was no fat there to protect the skin where the ass cheeks meets missy's legs on the side. It also left a much darker and meaner looking dark red welt.

Missy thought that the cane felt much different than the strap or the brush and provided both a sting at first and then a few seconds later, and a deep down hurt.

Missy thought that at first when the cane struck her ass, it felt like the sting like a bunch of bees stinging you. Then as that part calmed down a little, missy felt a deep down hurt as the pain settled in the muscle. That hurt did not seem to go away as fast.

Miss T apparently believed that the key to a good canning was to spread out the pain over a longer time frame and concentrate on make each and every stroke hurt the most which could be judged by the color and deepness of the welts.

Therefore, Miss T seemed to take her time and give one stroke every 10 to 15 seconds. It seemed to take the pain from any one stroke about that long to build up to the maximum pain level anyway.

Miss T seemed to accomplish two things by taking her time. Each stroke hurt the most

it could hurt and two, Miss T could build
the hurt like building a fire.

Miss T had several welts were hurting at
the same time that way while yet another
stroke would arrive, another welt would be
added. As the welts accumulated the pain
would likewise accumulate until missy ass
was becoming just one big mess of welts and
hurt.

Miss T stopped caning missy for a minute.
Miss T changed sides and started caning
missy again from the other side and all
missy could do was cry and cry and cry and
learn to be more obedient and in this case,
be more polite.

Missy knew that Miss T really enjoyed
punishing her and missy was really feeling
that punishment with Miss T's cane as stroke
after stroke after stroke and welt after
welt after welt caused more and more and
more pain to accumulate and missy could
just not take it. Missy just cried her eyes
out and hurt even more.

Miss T stopped after 50 strokes and left
missy there to cry and whimper and to hurt.
Missy could feel the welts, especially on
the side of her ass as they hurt and burned
and itched at the same time.

Missy thought that that caning was going
to have a long lasting effect as far as the

pain went as she thought that her ass would hurt for days if not a week or more.

Miss T left missy there to allow her some time to catch her breath from the first canning and the most severe punishment missy had ever received. It must have taken missy over five minutes to calm down. Miss T then helped missy to her feet, hooked her wrist cuffs behind her back again and told missy to kneel down.

As missy knelt down, missy knew that Miss T was going to tell her to give her the kiss of submission. Missy also knew that Miss T was going to judge how missy was feeling about Miss T by how much missy showed that she loved kissing Miss T's ass hole for her, or not.

As much as missy suffered thru that horrible caning and as much as missy cried and suffered some more, missy also knew that she was sorry that she disappointed Miss T and missy was going to give Miss T a better then ever kiss of submission to prove it.

Missy figured that would tell Miss T that missy accepted responsibility for her sin and acknowledged that she deserved to be punished as Miss T saw fit. Missy could not convey that message as well with words at that time and both Miss T and missy knew it.

Miss T turned her ass towards missy and pulled her tight skirt up around her waist and lowered her panties to her knees. Miss T took both her lovely ass cheeks, one with each hand, and spread them so missy could get her face between them.

Missy took a deep breath and stuck her face all the way between Miss T ass cheeks and kissed and kissed and kissed Miss T's ass hole. Missy then licked Miss T's hole like it was the best tasting thing in the world and missy was starving.

Miss T realizing that missy did not seem to be stopping and told missy that was enough. Missy made sure she licked up any extra saliva before pulling her face out and gave Miss T one last big kiss.

Miss T told missy to get up and to get back to work. Miss T asked if anyone else wanted corner time from missy and both Miss Jill and Miss Beth spoke up and said yes.

Alright missy sometime after dinner this evening you stand in each of Miss Jill's and Miss Beth's corners for 15 minutes each to conclude your punishment. Yes Miss, thank you Miss, curtsey.

Missy needed to get back to work as she was getting farther and farther behind. So missy took her sore ass and went to wash her face and fix her makeup and get to work.

However, I was sure that both missy and Miss T got the same message; which was that missy seemed willing and actually happy to submit to Miss T's rule of the house.

After missy cleaned the kitchen for the last time that evening she went to Miss Jill's room first. Missy knocked on the door frame as the doors in the house were left open most of the time.

Miss Jill; would not be a convenient time for me to stand in the corner for you, curtsey. Yes, Missy, come on in, thank you Miss, curtsey.

Missy settled in the corner and set her timer for 16 minutes and lowered her panties to mid-thigh and hooked her wrist cuffs behind her back and tucked her dress up around her wrist cuffs so that her entire bare ass was on full display for Miss Jill, just the way Miss Jill wanted missy to stand in her corner.

While missy was standing in Miss Jill's corner she could not help but to think that she really felt strange and embarrassed to have to address my sister as Miss Jill. Such names seemed alright with missy for the other girls, but not for my sister.

Nevertheless, missy will need to address Miss Jill in that manner and missy will just need to get use to it, I thought. Missy also thought it was strange that she got an erection while standing in the corner for Miss Jill.

Missy, got erections when she stood in the corner for the other girls as well, but none of them were related to missy. Missy also noticed that her most intense erections came when she stood in the corner for Miss Beth and Miss T.

It seemed to missy that since Miss Beth and Miss T had a much greater interest and enjoyment of missy being punished and standing in the corner that for some reason knowing their feelings made missy even more excited, cock wise, to stand in the corner for them. That is not to say that missy understood any of that, rather she was just noticing differences among the different ladies.

A few minutes later missy could hear Miss Jill getting closer to her. Miss Jill used her hand to feel missy's ass and missy's welts. Miss Jill whispered in missy's ear that she could feel the welts with her hand as missy moaned a little in pain from Miss Jill's ungentle touch.

That cane must have really hurt you, missy, as those welts are really big and nasty looking. What was missy supposed to say, NO! They did not hurt, when in fact missy never felt such pain in her entire life. So, missy just said; yes Miss.

After Miss Jill played with and teased missy for a minute or two she left missy along to finish her corner time. The bell went off and missy un-hooked her wrist cuffs and pulled up her panties and smoothed her dress.

Missy looked over to Miss Jill and said, good night Miss, curtsey. Miss Jill gave missy a big smile and said good night as well.

Missy went down the hallway and knocked on Miss Beth's door frame and asked Miss Beth if it was a good time for her to have missy stand in her corner, curtsey.

Missy got a big smile from Beth as Beth told missy to come on in that she had been waiting for her. Yes Miss, as missy gave Beth a very friendly curtsey and walked over to the corner that Miss Beth likes missy to stand in.

However, as missy arrived at the corner and was about to lower her panties to stand in Miss Beth's corner the same way she stands in Miss Jill's corner, Miss Beth told missy to leave her panties up for the time being.

Miss Beth told missy that she was to stand in the corner just until Miss Beth finished her shower and then she wanted missy to lick her ass real nice for her like missy did the other night. Yes Miss, curtsey.

So, missy just stood in the corner and Miss Beth went and took a shower. Missy was pretty happy about Miss Beth's decision as missy would have preferred to kiss and lick and enjoy Miss Beth's ass then to stand in the corner any day.

Miss Beth came back about 10 minutes later and lay over the side of the bed and called missy. Missy turned around and said yes Miss, curtseyed to Beth and then got on her knees between Miss Beth's legs and just enjoyed the sight of Miss Beth's very nice shapely and plump ass.

Missy noticed a can of whipped cream on the floor next to Miss Beth's legs as Miss Beth told missy that the whipped cream was there for missy's use instead of missy using her own cream. Miss Beth meant that missy was not to masturbate on Miss Beth's ass and use missy's cum as the cream.

Missy began by kissing Miss Beth's ass all over her cheeks and even gave her a few hickies as missy did not really need any cream to enjoy Miss Beth's ass at all. Missy loved Miss Beth's ass just the way it was.

Nevertheless, missy picked up the can of whipped cream and sprayed some on Miss Beth's ass. Missy especially concentrated on getting the whipped cream down inside Miss Beth's cleft and used her finger to get some all around and inside Miss Beth's ass hole as missy did need the whipped cream to lubricate Miss Beth's ass hole so she could tongue fuck Miss Beth.

Missy began by enjoying all the whipped cream that was all over Miss Beth's fine ass cheeks and licked it all up and then even gave Miss Beth a few more hickies.

Then missy started to lick all the whipped cream out of Miss Beth's cleft as missy licked from the bottom to the top of Miss Beth's ass crack. With each lick missy would go deeper and deeper into Miss Beth's crack until missy had licked up all of the whipped cream.

By the time missy got around to licking up the whipped cream on Miss Beth's ass hole it melted and was just a gooey mess. Missy did not care about the whipped cream, she just needed something to lubricate Miss Beth's anus and the gooey whipped cream was fine.

So, missy used her hands to spread Miss Beth's ass cheeks a bit so that she could get her tongue down to Miss Beth's ass hole so she could to lick all around it.

Missy did not find that Miss Beth's ass hole had any flavor, but she did find that as she licked it for Miss Beth that Miss Beth seemed to love it as she squirmed all over the side of the bed and moaned up a storm for missy.

Finally missed used her tongue to poke it in and out of Miss Beth's ass hole and Miss Beth was going nuts with enjoyment as Miss Beth would tell missy OH!!!!! THAT'S IT MISSY! Oh!!! OH!!!! THAT'S IT MISSY!

Missy gave Miss Beth's ass hole a good tongue fucking and then Miss Beth told missy that was enough and missy stopped and leaned back on her haunches waiting to see if Miss Beth wanted anything else.

Beth just laid there for a minute and then told missy that she could return to the corner, only that time missy was to stand in the corner properly with her panties down by her mid-thighs and her hands cuffed behind her back and her dressed tucked up around her hands so that Miss Beth could get a good look at missy's well welted ass from missy's caning.

Missy stood up, yes Miss, curtseyed to Miss Beth and headed to the corner. As soon as missy was properly standing in the corner, Miss Beth was by her side using her hand to feel missy's welts just like Miss Jill did when missy was standing in Miss Jill's corner.

WOW! The welts really feel neat Miss Beth told missy. Missy did not say anything and was really embarrassed. However, at the same time, missy was sort of happy that she was pleasing Miss Beth even at missy's own expense.

Miss Beth went back and got up on her bed and missy could hear Miss Beth getting excited over and over again. Missy thought that Miss Beth had three orgasms that evening as she masturbated to the site of missy's well welted ass cheeks, as well as, Beth's obvious enjoyment of seeing missy stand in the corner.

However, that night Miss Beth also had the extra excitement of missy licking her ass so nice for her as well as the nice tongue fucking missy gave to Miss Beth's ass hole.

The bottom line for missy was that she felt like she was just being used as a play thing for Miss Beth to have a good time. Oddly, however, missy did not seem to mind and in fact maintained her rock hard erection throughout the entire time she was in Miss Beth's room.

Missy was only sorry that she was not permitted to masturbate to relieve her own excitement, but Miss T told missy that was against the rules and missy seemed to find enough trouble without even trying so she did not need to disobey Miss T on purpose.

Missy's time in the corner was over and after she un-hooked her wrist cuffs and

pulled up her panties and smoothed her dress
and said good night to Miss Beth and gave
Miss Beth a nice curtsey, missy went to bed
horny, but obedient to Miss T.

DRY CLEANERS HUMILIATION:

After enjoying a day off on Sunday to rest my feet and legs from a few more days of missy wearing those five inch high heels and working so many hours each day and especially standing in the corner for over an hour and a half on Saturday, I was very happy to rest and enjoy an nice quiet day by myself.

On Monday it was another day of classes. I had some trouble sitting still on my sore ass that missy got for me by earning that caning as apparently missy had not learned to be so obedient as of yet.

That cane really hurt and all those welts on my ass were still stinging and hurting when I would move around and especially when I tried to sit on them on those hard wood seats in the college classes.

Tuesday morning, as missy was getting dressed in the morning missy was telling herself that it was dry cleaner day again and missy needed to go there dressed as the sexy French maid and act like she does not care if everyone sees her or laughs at her.

Missy was telling herself that she cannot afford to get punished again. She needed to be obedient to Miss T. After all, Miss T deserved missy's obedience as Miss T has treated missy with complete respect and patience during missy's training.

In addition, missy really liked Miss T. Yes, I know that I am talking to myself about missy, but I needed the motivation for missy to go out in public again. Funny, missy is the one who goes out in public as a sexy French maid, but, I am the one who gets embarrassed.

Missy went into everyone's room and picked up all the dry cleaning bags and slowly dragged herself to the car for the ride she was most not looking forward to. Missy took her good old time driving over to the dry cleaners. One might have thought that missy was an old lady she drove so slowly.

As missy drove that morning she could still feel the pain in her ass from all of the welts that were still itching and throbbing. MAN! Missy thought, that caning really hurt and if she could avoid another caning she would be much happier.

Missy arrived at the shopping center and missy knew that she had to get out of the car. But, the car door for some reason was not opening by itself. After missy just sat there for a few minutes trying to get up the courage to get out and go into the shop, missy finally opened the door and got out and opened the back door and gathered up all of the bags of clothes and missy made her way to the shop. Missy surveyed the parking lot and it was quiet without much traffic at that time.

Missy walked thru the parking lot while walking closely against the parked cars so she was "less" out in the open. Missy got to the front door and looked inside thru the glass door and saw that there were two other people in the shop.

Missy held the 6 bags of clothes in front of her to cover herself the best she could and pushed the door open and walked inside. The store owner, Miss Nancy, saw missy come in and gave her a big smile, while the other two ladies were facing the counter and did not see missy.

Missy waited in line while the other two ladies completed their business and they both left not really noticing missy as missy continued to hold the 6 bags in front of her and just looked at the floor. Meanwhile another lady came into the store and stood behind missy.

The lady behind missy could obviously see missy's maid dress with the super short hem line and the big apron bow in the back. She also had a good look at missy's nice legs along with missy's nice ass holding out the back of the dress in a very sexy manner. Missy felt an inflow of embarrassment as her face was getting hotter.

Missy moved up to the counter and Miss Nancy again smiled at missy as missy put the 6 bags on the counter. Once missy's hands were emptied and as she felt like crying from humiliation, missy nevertheless stepped back one step from the counter and said good morning Miss Nancy and gave Miss Nancy a nice curtsey and a nice smile.

The lady behind missy could not help but see missy curtsey to Miss Nancy. Then missy heard an "OH MY!" from behind her and missy's face seemed to get even hotter from embarrassment.

Missy waited until Miss Nancy checked in all the new bags. Then Miss Nancy went to get the clean clothes for missy. Meanwhile another lady came into the shop and now missy had two ladies standing behind her.

Miss Nancy came back with the six previous bags and the clean clothes on hangers and put the bags on the counter and hung the clothes on a hanging rod next to the counter for missy to take.

But, before missy picked up anything she thanked Miss Nancy, gave her another nice curtsey and another nice smile and told her to have a nice day. As missy was picking up all of her stuff, she heard the one lady behind her say to the other lady, "did you see that?"

The other lady said she was speechless. Missy picked up all of her stuff and left the shop, however as she needed to pass the two ladies to get out of the shop missy looked at the floor so she did not have to make eye contact with either of them.

Later that day, Miss T questioned missy about her trip to the shop and missy basically told Miss T the story I just told you. Miss T told missy that from now on that missy is not allowed to look at the ground and that she needed to keep her head up and be proud of who she is.

Miss T told missy that she needed to acknowledge the other people by smiling at them and saying hello yes Miss, curtsey. Missy thought that that was a real tough ask. However, missy also knew that she needed to obey Miss T, or find another place to live. Yes Miss, curtsey.

Missy was not sure why her job included all of that humiliation in public? Missy was not sure if Miss T was making missy embarrass herself like that in public because Miss T like it or if it excited Miss T. Or, perhaps, Miss T was teaching missy something that missy has not realized just yet.

Then, maybe, just maybe it was all of the above.

MOM CAME TO VISIT:

Saturday while missy was busy cleaning the kitchen the doorbell rang and missy needed to go answer it again. That was about the fifth time missy needed to answer the front door. Each and every other time missy found the experience to be quite embarrassing.

Missy understood that answering the door was part of her job. However, it seemed to be one part that she really did not like. Missy never knew who was going to be on the other side of the door and missy found that somewhat nerve racking as she was afraid that it may be someone she had met in college and they may recognize her.

Nevertheless, it really did not matter who was there as missy needed to answer the door anyway, so knowing did not matter all that much when you think about it. Missy just thought that she would prefer to know then to be surprised. Or, better yet not have to answer the door at all. Alright, enough of missy's wining to herself.

Missy opened the door and found Mom there. Or, should I say missy saw my mother on the other side of the door. Missy gets confused sometimes as to whether her relationship with people is with her or with me.

As missy had been told to do, missy looked at my mother and said, good morning Ma'am, I am maid missy, how may I help you? curtsey. My Mom smiled and told missy that she was there to check on her children and see how they were doing.

Missy asked Mom to follow her and showed her to the living room. Missy asked my Mom to have a seat and asked Mom if she wished to have a cold drink? Mom gave missy a big smile and said no thank you. Missy then said, if you will excuse me, Ma'am, I will go and get your daughter, curtsey, and missy left the room.

While missy was going upstairs to get my sister, Jill, she was thinking about how much she appreciated Mom going along with what Mom just saw as missy has never been in front of Mom with her completed sissy maid look. Missy was also thinking about how humiliated she was to be looking like that and having to curtsey to my Mom.

Missy found Jill in the office and told her that Mom was there to see them and looked at Jill as if to ask, could she change back into some of my male clothes for this visit.

Jill just said lets go and did not really give missy a chance to say anything.

Missy followed Jill, back to the living room and Jill gave Mom a big hung and said that it was great to see her. Mom moved over and gave missy a big hug also and told missy that it was great to see her too.

Mom also said, by the way missy, you really look very pretty. Thank you Ma'am, curtsey. I really like the curtsey part too missy, you seem very polite and very obedient, Mom added. Thank you Ma'am, curtsey.

Missy felt a little better as Mom seemed to be accepting missy as she was.

Mom told us to have a seat, here missy Mom said, you sit next to me, yes Ma'am, curtsey. Missy sat down on the couch next to Mom. Jill sat across from them in a lounge chair.

Missy needed to make sure that she sat properly with her knees together and her legs bent back to the side so Miss Jill could not see her up her dress and see her panties. Missy certainly did not want to give Miss Jill any reason to have missy punished while Mom was there for a visit.

Mom asked Jill about my duties and training so far and overall Miss Jill gave Mom a good report and added that missy was learning fast and missy seemed very submissive to Miss T and with her training, just as you said she would, Mom.

WHAT?????? I thought!!!!!! WHAT????? Just like you said Mom???? Then missy thought, does that also mean that Mom knows about missy's kiss of submission and missy's other ass eating services? As missy was thinking such thoughts she started to get more and more embarrassed. Missy did not like thinking Mom knew that missy enjoyed licking the girl's asses.

Missy stopped her daydreaming as Mom looked over to missy and said, with the makeup and the wig, missy, you do look just like a real girl, thank you Ma'am. Oddly, missy was so happy to hear that as Mom was the third person that month who thought that missy looked like a real girl and for some reason that pleased missy.

Mom asked missy how she was feeling about her new self. Missy was too embarrassed to tell her Mom about the punishments she had received so far, or the ass service she had provided. So missy just told Mom that overall she has enjoyed being missy and she enjoyed being trained by Miss T. That Miss T was a real fine lady, just you are Ma'am.

Good, Mom said, how about if the three of us go out for lunch. Missy was about to panic as in, NO WAY! NO HOW! Missy did not want to go out with anybody anywhere dressed as a French maid.

However, either to save missy from that high level of humiliation or maybe Mom and Jill did not want to go out with missy dressed like a French maid, but in either case, Miss Jill looked at missy and said that she would give missy something else to wear.

Missy thought, WHAT? Does that mean they are going to make missy go out dressed as a girl, but just not like a French maid? Are Miss Jill and Mom going to make missy go out to a public restaurant dressed as a girl?

Missy thought about it and figured that for the time it takes for her to take off all her makeup and turn back into me would take while. Then when we got back missy would have to re-apply her makeup and get all dressed again, so it did make sense for her just to change into something more acceptable for a girl her age.

But still? Going out in public dressed as a girl? Missy did not like the idea, but then again, missy knew in the end that she would do what she was told to do by Mom and or Miss Jill. Missy was remembering the first rule "OF MOM", OBEDIENCE!!!!!!!!! In fact, as missy thought about it, that was Mom's only rule, Obedience!

Miss Jill told missy to follow her and missy got up and said yes Miss, curtsey, and followed Miss Jill to Jill's bedroom. Miss Jill picked out a light blue satin blouse and a short white pleaded tennis skirt for herself.

Miss Jill thought for a minute and told Missy to go and put on her original maid outfit, which was the one with the black satin blouse and the black flared skirt. Miss Jill said that outfit would look better with missy's black high heels and her white short lacy socks yes Miss, curtsey.

Missy went to her room and put on the clothes Miss Jill told her to wear and changed into her long wig as well. All the time was getting more and more nervous as every minute ticked by. Missy had not left the house as a female except for those trips to the dry cleaners and they were embarrassing enough but they were not like being out in public, with other people, where it is crowded.

However, as nervous as missy was feeling, she also had a sense of excitement about her as she enjoyed wearing those sexy female clothes. Missy had even looked forward one day, in her fantasies, to going out in public dressed as a girl. But, with her mother? That was not part of any fantasy and was just making missy feel more embarrassed.

When missy returned to the living room wearing her other clothes and her new long sexy wig, both Mom and Jill gave her big smiles and told her she looked great. The three of them walked out the back door to the car. Mom told missy to drive and that she would sit in the back with Jill.

Missy opened the car door for them and closed it before walking around to the driver's side. Missy looked like the chauffeur and even acted like a chauffeur.

Mom told Missy where to go and she followed Mom's directions and drove about 15 minutes before Mom told her to pull in to a restaurant. Missy parked the car and got out and went and opened the door for the two ladies to get out and the three of them walked into the restaurant.

Missy followed behind Mom and Jill as she still felt not only humiliated to be dressed like a sexy girl out in public, but with Mom.

The restaurant was made to look like a rundown old time sailing ship. The inside was decorated in that theme of the inside of the ship. So, it was somewhat darker inside then with most day time restaurants would be which was good for missy as she felt that she would be less conspicuous.

So far so good missy thought as she felt that no one was paying any particular attention to her. After all, my sister, Jill, was a beautiful sexy girl and missy was sure that she would gather a lot of attention anywhere she went.

Then missy was thinking that Mom was only 42 years old and had a real nice figure and was very nice looking herself, so she must get a lot of male attention herself. Mom did not dress her age either, as she was wearing a short skirt and high heels and a nice silk blouse and she still had her youthful long hair as well.

Missy thought that Mom still looked like a real catch at her age. Mom had a nice figure and had nice shapely legs with what seemed like a nice plump ass that stuck out the back of her skirt. Mom also had a very nice smile and bright cheerful face.

Mom chose a table in the corner so it was obviously not her intention to humiliate missy, rather just to have a nice lunch with her children. The three of them ordered lunch and then missy realized that she needed to get up and go to the salad bar.

The three of them went together but missy's tummy was jumping all around as she would be under bright lights right there in public where everyone could see her as the salad bar was lite up pretty well.

Missy just tried to get her salad and not look at anybody and that seemed to be working as she got back to the table without incident. But, missy then thought, what was she expecting?

The worse that could happen was that people would stare at her and maybe comment about her clothes. Or, could they tell that missy was really a guy? Missy was not sure, just a mess of thoughts in missy's head.

As missy looked around to see who was looking at her, missy did notice that although many of the guys took a look at her, they also took a good look at Miss Jill and even Mom. So, missy was thinking that she was just getting that attention as she looked real good in that short skirt and those five inch high heels. For some reason, that seemed alright with missy.

The three of them were eating their salads and chatting about their class schedules and class subjects and what they thought about being in college. Then Mom asked missy about her cleaning and how she scheduled everything and how everyone treats her.

Odd missy, thought, Mom calling me missy. Missy told Mom that there was a lot of work, but she had three full days a week to get it all done and that seems to be enough as long as she keeps at it and gets all her school work finished on the other four days.

Then Mom asked missy if she had been punished by Miss T and missy turned all red and told Mom about the spanking and the strapping and her disobedience at the dry cleaners.

Missy added the part about the caning for being rude to Miss Ida. So, Mom that was three times I was punished in just the first month. Mom, my ass still hurts a little from that caning and that was last Saturday.

Missy was asked about any additional punishments like corner time? Missy needed to confess that she was required to stand in all the girls' corners if they wanted her to after each punishment.

Missy continued to say that only Miss Beth, Miss Jill, and Miss T seemed to be interested in having her stand in their corners and the other four did not seem to show any interest in missy other than to watch her get spanked or strapped and do all their housework and laundry.

After some more questions from Mom, missy said that she was expected to walk and sit and stoop down like a lady and although she had found that to be a real challenge sometimes that she thought she was getting the hang of it.

After a few more question from her Mom, missy had to admit that she has fantasized about going out in public dressed like a girl and that she loved wearing her maid clothes at home and does enjoy cleaning for all of the girls and trying to please them.

Missy? Mom asked; if there were some other parts of you punishment you did not tell me about? Missy turned all red from embarrassment again but after a long pause, told her Mom about the kiss of submission that she and to give to Miss T, Miss Beth, and that guy, Ken.

Mom asked missy if she liked that part. Missy got even a redder face as she confessed to her Mom and Miss Jill that she liked it with both Miss T and Miss Beth as they have very nice asses. But, more importantly, missy added, they both seemed to really enjoy it and missy felt very good about being able to please them.

So, Mom asked me, have you dated any of those college girls yet? No, Mom, I really have not had time with all the class work and all the maid work. Sunday is my only real day off and so far I have enjoyed doing nothing but hanging around the house, going to the gym, and watching some tennis or football on TV.

The three "ladies" enjoyed the rest of their lunch and drove back to the house as missy needed to get back to work. Mom and Jill went shopping.

DRY CLEANER TUESDAY:

Once again I enjoyed a nice Sunday off and enjoyed watching some football. My legs did not seem all that tired that Sunday as for the third week in a row missy only needed to wear her high heels for three days that week and more importantly missy did not need to stand in the corner at all that last week as missy finally managed to get past a week without getting herself punished for something.

Monday was just another easy day of college classes and missy staying in her room in the evening enjoying the peace and quiet of being by alone.

Tuesday, missy was again on her way to the dry cleaners. Missy was more nervous than ever before as missy was remembering Miss T's new rules about missy needing to hold her head up and to smile at everyone and to say hello to everyone and act like she was proud to be Miss T's sexy French maid. Missy was telling herself that it could not be much worse than last week but

missy knew that would depend on how many
people she saw.

 That day as missy was walking in the
parking lot going to the shop she passed
one lady who was going to her car and missy
managed a smile and said good morning,
Ma'am. The lady responded in kind and they
both moved on.

When missy entered the shop there again
were two ladies in line at the counter. The
shop owner, Miss Nancy, saw missy come in
and smiled at her and missy in turn smiled
back and said good morning, Miss.

Missy got in line behind the two ladies
and then missy got upset when a man walked
into the shop and came up behind her. Missy
thought that being a sexy French maid in
front of those ladies was bad enough, but
in front of a man, missy's face became flush
with blood as her humiliation level was
rising quickly. After all, the last man who
saw missy at the dry cleaners stared her
down and then offered her a job.

The two ladies left and missy knew that
she was going to have to curtsey to the shop
owner right there in front of that man. For
some reason missy was so much more afraid
and nervous curtseying in front of a man.

Nevertheless, missy did place all her
things on the counter and took a step back

and said good morning Miss, smiled, and gave Miss Nancy a nice curtsey.

Missy then heard the man say; well, that was different, do you curtsey like that to everyone? Missy turned around, and as much as she did not want to, yes Sir, curtsey. Well, that's really neat, why do you do that, The man asked? It is a sign of respect, missy responded. Yes, the man said, I understand that, but why do you do it? It is required of me by my Miss T, Sir.

Oh really, you have a Miss T and do you always do what Miss T tells you to do, no matter what? Yes Sir. So you always obey your Miss T, the man asked again? Yes Sir, curtsey.

Why, the man asked? Missy responded that she works for Miss T and therefore Miss T in entitled to her obedience. So you get paid to dress like a whore and do whatever your Miss T tells you to do, the man asked again? Yes Sir, curtsey.

Just then another lady walked into the shop and missy moved over from in front of the counter as to not be in the lady's way and the man moved over with her. But, missy made sure that she smiled at the lady and said good morning to her as well.

However, the man was not letting go of missy. Well isn't that interesting the man

said? Do you enjoy working for your Miss T
or are you just desperate for the job, the
man asked? Yes Sir, I enjoy working for Miss
T very much.

So do you always dress this sexy for
your Miss T or do you do it to attract men?
The man asked? Missy told the man that yes
she always dresses that way and she does
it because her Miss T requires it and not
because she is looking to attract men.

Well that's all very interesting the man
said, by the way, are you available if I
wanted to hire you and pay you more then you
make now? Missy assumed that the question
was really his way of asking her if he could
he take her home and fuck her.

Missy was thinking about how surprised he
would be when he found out what missy really
was. You know a sexy French maid with a
penis. Missy told the man that she was happy
in her present position and could not think
of any reason to change, especially not for
money, Sir, curtsey.

Well, thank you for your time young lady
and have a nice day and the man left the
shop. Missy thought that was strange as he
only spoke to her and conducted no business.
Missy turned to the shop owner, pick up her
things, said thank you, gave Miss Nancy a
nice smile and a nice curtsey and left the
shop.

As soon as missy left the shop she saw
Miss T sitting on the bench outside the shop
and missy's heart skipped a beat as Miss T
was sitting next to the man that was just
quizzing missy. Miss T called missy over to
her.

Missy went over to Miss T. Miss T told
missy to put everything in the car and to
come back as she would wait there on the
bench for her, yes Miss. Missy could not
curtsey with all the stuff she was carrying
and Miss T understood as much, so missy
was permitted not to curtsey under such
circumstances.

Missy was about as nervous as she ever
has been as she walked back to the car that
morning as missy was just trying to figure
out if she disobeyed Miss T in any way
that would end up with her being punished.
Missy would have hated to humiliate herself
that much in one morning and still get
punished.

Additionally, on missy's way back to Miss
T, missy had to walk across the parking lot
without the benefit of any clothes and or any
bags to hold in front of her to cover herself
enough to at least provide her with some
sense of protection from total humiliation
of being dressed that way. Additionally,
the back of missy's dress kept blowing in
the wind giving a few guys a good look at
her panties.

Miss T always seemed to find a way to make things more embarrassing for missy. Now, missy knew that she needed to stand on the sidewalk in her full sexy French maid uniform while she spoke with Miss T and missy had no idea how long that would take. Missy was also even more embarrassed to be there in front of the man that was still sitting there on the bench with Miss T.

Missy returned to the bench where Miss T and that man were sitting and said, yes Miss, curtsey as missy's face burned bright again with embarrassment having to curtsey right there on a public side walk. But, missy managed to look at the man also and curtsey to him as well as missy was surly not looking for any trouble.

Miss T told missy that this gentleman was telling her all about this maid that he met in the dry cleaners and he tells me that I am so lucky to have such a well behaved and obedient maid. He even tells me that he tried to buy you away from me and that you told him that you were happy where you are.

Missy, I really appreciate the excellent report. So, missy, I am going to give you are real treat tonight and let you lick my pussy for me. You are dismissed. Missy again curtseyed to Miss T and then to the man and took her leave.

Missy walked back to her car and could not believe how humiliated she was to be told in front of that man that she was going to have to lick Miss T's pussy that night. Then as missy thought about it, she wondered what it would be like to lick Miss T's pussy as she had never done such a thing before and really did not even have any idea as to what to do.

When missy got in her car she almost cried as she was so proud that she could please Miss T and that Miss T was happy with her. That seemed like it made the whole totally humiliating morning alright with missy.

Oddly, missy did not seem happy or even think about not getting punished, rather her happiness for pleasing Miss T was paramount in missy's mind.

As missy was cleaning that afternoon she was thinking about what Miss T told her about getting to lick Miss T's pussy that night. I had no such experience and was not really sure what to do. Missy assumed that Miss T already knew that and would teach missy what to do.

Missy also wondered if Miss T knew that man in the dry cleaners as he did not conduct any business in there. He just came in and spoke with missy and left. So, missy thought that Miss T sent him in there just to test missy.

What that told missy was that anytime she
ever meet a stranger that she would never
know if that person was a friend of Miss T's
or really just a stranger?

Missy thought that it would certainly
make her think twice about how she reacts to
strangers in the future. Missy thought that
it was very cleaver of Miss T to set things
up that way so missy would just never know
when someone she sees knows Miss T or not.

MISS T'S PUSSY LICKING LESSON:

Later that evening Miss T called missy into her room and asked missy if she had every licked a pussy before. Missy was pretty sure that Miss T knew that missy had not, but answered her politely anyway with a no Miss, curtsey. Well, Miss T said; tonight, missy, I will teach you how to really please a woman, yes Miss, curtsey.

Missy never really gave much thought to licking anyone's pussy before and was not really looking forward to it. However, missy never thought about licking an ass before and that turned out to be something that missy was happy to do for Miss T. So, licking Miss T' pussy may be nice also, missy thought. Regardless, Miss T was not asking missy, she was telling missy and missy knew she would obey Miss T.

Miss T started to take off her clothes. However Miss T took them off real slow as if she was teasing missy and perhaps she was.

Nevertheless, missy had a rock hard cock even before Miss T had her bra off. Missy got to see Miss T's very fine firm breasts for the very first time.

Missy's exciting view of Miss T's breasts was interrupted as missy refocused her attention to Miss T's pussy as Miss T unzipped her skirt and slowly slid her skirt down to her ankles and stepped out of it and kicked the skirt to the side.

Missy's eyes were focused directly on Miss T's panties as she could not wait to see Miss T's pussy. Miss T looked at missy and could see the lust on her face as Miss T slowly removed her panties and let missy's eyes get a good look at her pussy area.

As missy had no experience with black girls, missy was a little surprised at to how black Miss T's pussy hair was, but none the less, missy loved what she saw. Miss T had a very neat but full triangle of pussy hair that made missy want to cum right there and then.

Miss T lay down on her bed and told missy to crawl up between her legs and put her face right up to Miss T's pussy and just stop and sniff it for a minute, yes Miss, curtsey.

Missy did as she was told and crawled up between Miss T's legs as she could not

take her eyes off Miss T's pussy. Missy
sniffed Miss T's pussy as she was told
and although missy thought that it did not
smell good, it did not smell bad either,
just unusual.

Alright missy, move back a little. As
missy did move back a little, Miss T sat up
and told missy that she was going to show
her the parts of a pussy and how missy has
to lick them all, but differently.

Miss T used her hands to show missy that
the pussy lips really had two layers. Missy
needed to lick the outside of the outer
lips; the inside of the inside lips, and in
between the two sets of lips as well. Then
Miss T showed missy where her clit was and
explained to missy what to do with it when
missy gets there with her tongue.

Miss T laid back down and told missy to
start to just use her lips on the inside
of her thighs and slowly lick up and down
the inside of her thighs just below her
beautiful pussy lips and Miss T moaned just
a bit as missy did so.

Missy did the same on Miss T's other
thigh and Miss T wiggled just a bit more.
Then Miss T told missy to start to kiss her
gently all along the inside of her thighs
alternating between the right and the left,
the left and the right and Miss T moaned
some more.

Then Miss T told missy to slowly move her mouth up towards Miss T's pussy and start to kiss and lick the outside of her pussy lips, first the right side and then the left side, kissing and licking and licking and gently licking and kissing.

Miss T told missy to move to the inside of her pussy lips and began kissing and licking and licking and kissing both the outside and the inside of each lip. Missy did so and that really got Miss T to wiggle a lot. As missy continued missy had Miss T moaning a lot more. Miss T even flopped her head back and forth from side to side a little.

Miss T told missy that she was doing fine but to lick more strongly. Missy started to lick Miss T's pussy lips a little stronger and licked from the bottom of Miss T's pussy to the top of her pussy like an ice cream cone. Missy was getting even more of a reaction out of Miss T that way as Miss T started to squirm more, moan more and even moved her hips around a little.

Missy could feel that Miss T's pussy was getting all wet and was developing an even stronger scent. Missy was not sure what all that was about as Miss T did not explain the wetness part to her. Nevertheless, missy just continued to obey Miss T and figured that she would find out about all that wetness later.

Miss T told missy that she needed to lick her pussy deeper and deeper a little at a time until missy could not lick any deeper. Missy kept up what she was doing and then she started going deeper and deeper with her tongue inside Miss T's pussy lips. Missy continued to lick deeper with each lick until she could not get her tongue inside of Miss T's pussy any deeper.

By then missy was pushing her entire face into Miss T's pussy and missy licked Miss T a bit more while moving her head back and forth back and forth like a tiger tearing apart a piece of meat. Missy was not sure why she did that, but Miss T liked it so missy kept it up.

Miss T told missy told move her tongue up to the very top of her pussy until missy felt her clit with missy's tongue. Missy started to lick around Miss T's clit but did not touch it yet. Missy sort of sensed that she was exciting Miss T and at the same time frustrating her and that seemed good to missy.

Miss T did not say anything anymore and missy assumed that Miss T was both testing her and at the same time enjoying the licking. Miss T broke her silence by simply saying NOW missy! NOW missy!

Missy immediately started licking her tongue all over Miss T's clit like she was a cat licking up milk and Miss T exploded all over missy's face in wave after wave after wave of juicy liquid that had a stronger scent than before.

Finally Miss T just nudged missy's head with her hand. Missy laid her head on the inside of Miss T's thigh and just stayed there with Miss T until Miss T told missy what else to do. Oh missy! Oh missy! That was great!

Missy assumed that all that liquid was cum, only not white cum like missy discharges when she cums. Missy was still not thrilled with the scent, but figured that she would get use to it over time if Miss T wanted missy to keep licking her pussy for her into the future.

About three minutes later, Miss T seemed calm again and started to very lightly scratch at the top of her pussy hair which missy took as a signal that she was ready for more. Missy looked up at Miss T and Miss T told missy to go ahead and do everything again, yes Miss.

Missy was a little more aggressive from the start the second time as she seemed to know she did a good job for Miss T the first time. Missy had Miss T moaning much louder the second time and had Miss T wiggling much more the second time and missy even had Miss T bucking her hips more the second time.

However, missy also noticed the second time that Miss T's pussy was soaking wet and Miss T's juices were getting all over missy's face. Missy was not happy about the sloppy mess, but missy kept doing what she was told and Miss T seemed to be enjoying herself even more the second time.

Missy seemed to have more confidence in her ability to please Miss T and Miss T seemed like she was happier the second time as she knew that missy was able to please her the first time. That second time, in less than two minutes missy had Miss T coming again as Miss T started another wave after wave after wave of orgasmic delight.

Once more when Miss T was finished she pushed missy's head away very gently and missy again rested her head on the inside of Miss T's thigh waiting to find out if Miss T wanted another or if Miss T was finished.

Missy was not sure what to expect, after all, when missy cums that was the end of the sex, at least for a while. Missy did not know if it was the same for women but she assumed that if she just obeyed Miss T she would find out.

A few minutes later Miss T signaled missy again and missy went back to work for the third time and again for a fourth time before Miss T was finished. Each time missy experienced a sloppier and sloppier Miss T pussy as it was getting wetter and wetter all the time.

Again, missy was not happy about smashing her face in that sopping wet pussy, but on the other hand Miss T seemed to love it and that was more important to missy than what missy seemed to like.

Alright Miss T said, that was great, just great, I'm finished now, clean me. Missy looked up at Miss T and just said, clean you? Missy was confused as to what Miss T wanted missy to do.

Miss T smiled and told missy, yes missy, now lick up all my juices. Yes Miss, and missy spent the next five minutes licking up as much of Miss T' pussy juice. However, missy thought that she was waging a losing battle as it seemed the more she licked up, the more juice that Miss T's pussy produced.

It seemed that Miss T understood that as she told missy to stop even though there seemed like an endless amount of pussy juice left still. Miss T told missy to move over while she turned over.

Miss T placed a pillow under her hips and told missy to clean her ass was well, yes Miss. Missy licked and sucked on Miss T's beautiful ass crack for longer than it took to lick up all of Miss T's pussy juice that leaked to Miss T's ass area.

But, missy did not care as she was having such a good time. Miss T noticed and told missy to finish up and missy dove into Miss T's crack with her tongue and licked Miss T's ass hole clean as well and then withdrew.

Miss T dismissed missy and missy said good night Miss and gave Miss T a nice curtsey and went to her room for the night.

WRONG FACE AND
A SPANKING:

It was just a normal Thursday morning and missy had a lot of cleaning and a lot of laundry to do as she does each Thursday. Missy had been getting along fine with getting all the laundry and all the cleaning done on her three days per week over her first month as the houses maid.

As well, missy had been doing very well in college on the other three days a week that she attended classes and did her school work. On Sunday's missy had been staying in her small apartment and resting and watching football on Sunday afternoons.

That Sunday missy was thinking that she has come to really enjoy dressing in her girl clothes very much. Missy was finding that she liked being dressed as a girl so much that she even considered going out sometimes in her wig and makeup and dressed as a girl. However, with the exception of that one time

with Mom and Jill when missy had no choice
in the matter, missy had not.

Anyway, missy just finished getting
herself a snack for lunch when the doorbell
rang. Missy still had not become comfortable
answering the door, but she did as it was
part of her job. Miss T was the only one
home that afternoon besides missy as Miss T
had a class cancel as the professor was ill
that day.

Missy reluctantly went to answer the door.
Missy opened the door a saw a fine looking
young lady standing there. In fact, as bad
luck would have it, her name was Betty and
she played tennis on the tennis club team at
the same club where I played tennis.

Good afternoon, my name is maid missy, how
may I help you, curtsey. Well, are you not
a pretty and polite maid? I am here to see
Tara. Yes Miss, please come in and have a
seat and I will get her for you, curtsey.

As Betty sat down on the couch, missy
asked her if she wanted to cold drink and
she declined. I will go and get Miss T for
you Miss, curtsey.

Missy went to go and get Miss T and Miss
T was all smiles. Miss T asked missy if she
thought that Betty recognized her from the
tennis club. Missy told Miss T that she was
not sure, but missy did not think so.

Alright missy, Betty and I are going out to lunch and will see you when we come back, yes Miss, curtsey. Miss T and Betty went out to lunch and missy continued her cleaning and laundry for the day as she had much to do that day just as missy had a lot to do every day to keep up behind 7 girls.

Miss T and Betty came back about an hour and a half later. When missy noticed they were home she found them in the living room just chatting away and smiling and having a good time.

Missy went and asked if she could get them any refreshments? Yes missy, Miss T replied, we would like some chocolate ice cream with whipped cream and a coke. Yes Miss, curtsey.

Missy went off to the kitchen to find that all of the ice cream had been eaten. Missy went back and told Miss T that there was no more ice cream. Alright missy, then I you need to go down to the Dairy Queen and get each of us a chocolate milkshake instead.

Missy hesitated a bit and sort of made a face showing that she was unhappy with that instruction. Miss T noticed right away that missy did not say yes Miss and curtsey and smile. To make things worse, Miss T noticed that Betty saw missy's face of unhappiness also.

Missy, I gave you and order! Yes Miss, curtsey. MISSY? Yes Miss, curtsey? When you get back, while we enjoy our chocolate milkshakes, you will stand in the corner and then you will get a spanking for that sour face and your lack of obedience. Yes Miss, curtsey and off missy went to the Dairy Queen.

Missy drove to the dairy queen and had to stand in line behind two others, one young women and one young man. Missy thought that they were on a date.

Anyway, the guy happened to turn around and saw missy walk up behind them. He kept turning around to look at missy. After he turned around for the third time, his girlfriend turned around and gave missy a good long look over. She shook her head in disgust and made a face like she thought missy was a whore.

Her boyfriend turned around again to look at missy and the girl smacked him on the arm and said, WHAT ARE YOU LOOKING AT????

Missy thought that it was a good thing that their ice cream showed up or they may have gotten in a fight as the guy still wanted to look at missy and his girlfriend was not happy with him.

Missy moved up to the window to order the two milkshakes. The young fellow behind the

window who could only see missy from above
the waist up actually leaned forward to get
a better look at missy. He gave missy a
big smile that both complimented missy and
embarrassed her at the same time.

When missy got back to the house, she
handed Miss T and Miss Betty their milkshakes
and just went and put her wrist cuffs on and
took herself over to corner and stood in the
corner to wait for her spanking.

Missy was pretty embarrassed in front
of that strange lady to be standing in the
corner. However, that did not stop missy
from getting an erection. In fact, missy
thought that it made her erection even
stronger. Missy did not understand why
being embarrassed gave her erections, it
just did.

Missy did not really understand anything
about her strange life. Why did missy enjoy
being missy? Why did I enjoy wearing girl's
clothes? I had no idea, missy had no idea,
we both sort of just did what we were told
to do by the women in our lives and we
seemed happy about it.

Anyway, as Miss T seems to like to do,
she finds a way to humiliate missy the most
she can in every situation and that upcoming
spanking was no exception.

When the ladies were finished their milkshakes, Miss T told missy to turn around and come over for her spanking. Missy un-hooked her wrist cuffs and turned around to give Miss T a yes Miss and a curtsey when she noticed that Miss Betty was sitting on the spanking chair with the spanking hairbrush in her hand instead of Miss T.

Missy guessed that they must have discussed who was going to spank missy while she was out at the dairy queen. Miss Betty called missy to her side, yes Miss, curtsey and missy went over and stood next to Miss Betty.

Missy was not really embarrassed to be spanked in front of Miss T as Miss T and missy had that type of relationship. However, missy was a lot more embarrassed to be spanked by Miss Betty.

Miss Betty was sitting there looking up at missy with a giant smile on her face that was telling missy that Miss Betty was about to have a great time.

Miss Betty smiled in a laughing manner as she reached up under missy's dress and started to lower missy's panties. However, Miss Betty noticed right away that she needed to pull the front of missy's panties away from missy's rock hard cock so that the panty band would clear missy's cock so that Miss Betty could lower them.

Miss Betty looked over to Miss T and they both had big smiles on their faces as they knew missy had an erection from thinking about getting a spanking from Miss Betty.

I still did not know what it meant that missy gets erections from being embarrassed or thinking about getting a spanking and I was not sure Miss Betty or Miss T knew any more than I did. However, that just seemed to be the way it was and Miss T and Miss Betty seemed to like knowing that missy had an erection for some reason.

Miss Betty tapped the hairbrush against her thigh and looked at missy and told missy that she knows what to do. Yes Miss, curtsey.

Missy lay over Miss Betty's lap. Miss Betty flipped missy's dress up over her hips and started spanking missy right away with real hard hairbrush spanks that had missy kicking her legs and yelling OUCH!!!!! right away.

Miss Betty was spanking missy real hard and real fast, about one spank every two seconds with no pattern other then pain and pain and more pain. As missy usually did when she got a spanking, she kicked her panties off right away involuntary as she kicked her legs up and down and screamed and yelled and acted just like a little girl.

Missy could not believe how much that hairbrush was hurting her ass. Miss Betty was spanking missy very hard and it was hurting far worse than missy had expected. For some reason, missy just assumed that Miss Betty would not be able to spank her as hard as Miss T. did.

However, missy was wrong as there was not much of a difference between a Miss T spanking and that Miss Betty spanking. They were like spanking twins; their spankings were hard to tell apart, not a good sign for missy. Missy guessed that Miss Betty must have had a lot of experience spanking someone to be able to handle a spanking so well.

All missy could do was kick her legs a little, bounce her head up and down and yell like the big sissy she was. Missy was trying to be tough and take the spanking a young man so that she would not be humiliated in front of Miss Betty any more then she had too.

However, that thought was not helping missy as the more spanks Miss Betty delivered the more missy moaned, the more missy ouched, the more missy kicked her legs, the more missy started to sob, as missy got a runny nose.

Miss Betty seemed to want to put on a good spanking show for Miss T. SPANK, SPANK,

SPANK!!!!!!!!! Missy had snot dripping out
of her nose, missy could not see anything
clearly as her tears were dripping from her
eyes as the spank total climbed towards 40
or 50 or maybe 60.

Miss Betty was getting into a nonstop
rhythm of SPANKING missy and SPANKING missy
and SPANKING!!!!!!!! Missy. Missy forgot
all about trying to be brave and take the
spanking like a young man as missy was taking
it just like the little sissy that missy
was. The humiliation was much worse than
missy had imagined as she was being spanked
very hard by a stranger.

Miss Betty spanked up one side of missy
ass and down the other side. Miss Betty
SPANKED missy and SPANKED missy and SPANKED
missy some more. Miss Betty SPANKED missy
up and down and back and forth from cheek
to cheek.

The   SPANKING,   SPANKING,   SPANKING,
SPANKING, SPANKING!!!!!!!!!!! continued. At
that point missy must have received around
100 Miss Betty hard spanks. Missy was crying
so hard and kicking her legs up and down
as Miss Betty was just pounded missy even
harder with that hairbrush.

The SPANKING continued as Miss Betty was
delivering a hard spank about every two
seconds, so the SPANKING has been going on
now for about three to four minutes. Miss

Betty just continued to SPANK missy and SPANK missy and SPANK!!!!!!!!!!! missy and SPANK!!!!!!! missy SPANK!!!! Missy until she had no struggle left in her and all.

Missy just lay limp across Miss Betty's lap and took the SPANKING!!!!!!!!!!!!!!!!!!! Missy was crying so hard.

Miss Betty finally stopped spanking missy after about 125 maybe 150 spanks later and about 6 or 7 minutes in time. Missy did not seem to have the strength to get off Miss Betty's lap as missy just laid there and cried and cried some more.

Missy continued to cry while she tried to get air though her mouth as her nose was clogged and was still dripping more snot. Miss Betty allowed missy to remain there over her lap for a minute or so and then Miss Betty helped missy off and told her to go back and stand in the corner, yes Miss, missy choked out thru her crying.

Miss T and Miss Betty sat on the couch behind missy for another 15 or 20 minutes while they watched missy stand in the corner like a naughty little school girl.

They chatted about all sorts of things, but one of those things was how much boys never seem to grow up and how they need strong women like them to keep them in line. Otherwise, the guy just become selfish and becomes good for nothing. I wondered what such young girls knew about men, after all, neither one of them were over 22 years old.

Miss Betty left and Miss T called me over to her. Yes miss, curtsey. Missy, I will only tell you this one time and I never expect to have to repeat myself.

Missy, if you ever embarrass me like that again in front of company, I will punish you so harshly that you may wish to leave this house. This time, Miss Betty sort of enjoyed your bad attitude as it gave her a reason to spank you, which is something she really enjoys.

However, missy, you were just lucky it was Miss Betty. If it had been someone else that you behaved like that in front of, I would have punished you like you have never been punished before.

DO YOU HEAR ME MISSY AND DO YOU UNDESTAND ME MISSY? Yes Miss, curtsey.

THE C.U.N.T.S.

The following week nothing worth mentioning happened. I went to classes on Monday, Wednesday, and Fridays. Missy worked on Tuesdays, Thursdays, and Saturdays and I had off on Sundays to do whatever I wanted.

Missy was getting use to all the yes Miss's and all the curtseying and all the girls were getting use to missy and everyone was getting along fine. Everyone, especially Miss T and Miss Beth seemed to appreciate all missy's good house work for them and there did not seem to be any complaints.

If missy could just get thru some embarrassing times and continue to serve the ladies well and remain obedient to Miss T, things seem like they will work out just fine for all concerned. After all the only downside for missy so far were the embarrassing times and those punishments. Missy just needed to avoid more punishments by behaving better.

Missy got to lick Miss T's ass and pussy again for her Tuesday night and missy really enjoyed herself. Miss Beth had missy lick her pussy for her on Thursday night and missy enjoyed that even more. When missy was finished Miss Beth told her that she could masturbate. When missy got back to my room, missy masturbated three times that night while she thought about Miss Beth's nice ass.

Saturday; apparently Miss Betty liked missy so much that Miss Betty asked Miss T if missy could serve for her at a party she was having at her house that afternoon with her tennis team.

Obviously I would not be telling you this story if Miss T did not agree to it and missy's fate was sealed. Missy was told by Miss T two things; first, that missy was to serve at the party. Second, missy was told in a very stern tone that Miss T expected missy to make Miss T proud of her maid and that missy had better not disappoint her!

I really did not think that was fair to me as I only agreed to be the sissy maid for the house in exchange for room and board. I never agreed to be lent out for the fun of others.

However, in the back of my mind, I always hear my Mom's voice at times like this. YOU WILL ALWAYS BE HAPPIER IF YOU OBEY THE WOMEN

IN YOUR LIFE. So, missy was going to obey Miss T and do what she wanted.

After all, missy also had another voice in her head and it was mine. My voice was telling missy that missy really like Miss T and if missy serving at Miss Betty's party would make Miss T happy and make Miss T look good then missy was willing to do it just to please Miss T. Missy wanted Miss T to be happy with her maid missy. Missy wanted Miss T to be proud of her maid.

Missy was told to wear her French maid outfit with the white ruffled top and long white sleeves with the middle and bottom parts being black. The dress was very short, like all of missy's maid uniforms, however that dress also had a full petticoat so it stick way out on the sides which made it look even shorter.

Missy wore her long black wig with the long bangs and that allowed the hair to hang half way down missy's back and also had several locks wrapping around her shoulders that hung in the front on both sides of her face. Missy wore her fishnet stockings and her white 5 inch heels, and of course a white apron.

Missy and to report to Betty's at 7:30 pm on Saturday night. Even while missy was driving over to Betty's house, I really wanted to object as being Miss T's and the

BITCHES maid and serving at someone else's
party is not the same thing. The other part
of me, missy, she wanted to make Miss T
happy even at missy's own humiliation.

Then, missy remembered the strapping she
got the last time missy tried to challenge
Miss T by wearing that raincoat to the dry
cleaners. Missy, again, just decided to do
as she was told by Miss T. Missy always just
seemed better off obeying then not obeying
or arguing with Mom, Miss Jill, Miss T, or
any of the BITCHES.

As you can imagine, for the last few days
leading up to that evening, just thinking
about it made missy very nervous pending
not only missy's humiliation but mine was
well as I had to assume that those ladies
would know who I really was.

Knowing Miss T, it was most likely that she
set missy up with Betty so missy's service
would be nonstop humiliation in every way
Miss T could think of. Miss T seemed to
really enjoy and get excited by missy's
embarrassing adventures and humiliations.

However, I found out later, as I got to
know and understand Miss T, that it was
not missy's humiliation that Miss T really
liked, rather it was missy's obedience. Miss
T enjoyed just the fact that missy would
obey her. Missy's blind obedience gave Miss

T a thrill and showing off missy's obedience to others increased Miss T's pleasure.

It was sort of Miss T's way of bragging and showing off that she had such a maid that was so obedient to her. Missy was certainly not something that anyone else seemed to have, so it sort of made Miss T a special person around campus and around the house. Missy was basically Miss T's ego trip.

Anyway, as I said, just thinking about that night caused me not to play tennis very well on Friday night. I spent too much time dwelling on Saturday night. I guess all the girls at the club would now know why I don't have any body hair and my legs look so nice in my very short tennis shorts.

Oh yea, there is one other thing you need to know before missy and I go to Betty's house. Missy found out that the "Guy" Ken, who gave missy that horrible strapping and who afterwards fucked Miss T in the ass when missy had to lick all of his cum out of Miss T's ass is the same guy that lives with Betty.

However, missy doesn't know if Betty knew that Ken fucked Miss T in the ass or not. Missy did not know if maybe it is alright with Betty or maybe it was not alright with Betty. Missy did not know what type of relationship everyone had.

The bottom line for missy was her concern that Ken would be there as that would make the party much more humiliating for missy. You know, doing missy things in front of a guy was just more humiliating for missy for some reason.

Anyway, as all of you know Saturday night did arrive. Missy was extra nervous about whether or not Miss T would make me get dressed in missy's maid dress at home and have missy drive over to Betty's house.

Or, would I be able to drive to Betty's house and get dressed over there? What the hell am I thinking; of course I will have to be missy and drive over to Betty's as missy.

It would just be too time consuming and complicated for me to change into missy at Betty's house, putting on missy's makeup and everything. Additionally, there was always that chance that the girls will not know that missy is also me. Hay, I can wish and be hopeful, right?

When Saturday night came alone, Miss T did make missy stay dressed as the maid. After all, missy was cleaning at home all day as the maid anyway. So, missy just had to change her maid uniform and off she went into an evening of the unknown.

Missy drove about 10 minutes to get to Betty's house. Missy parked in the driveway and walked up to the front door. At that time of year it was almost dark by 7:30 pm, so missy was not all that concerned about being seen by others while she was outside of Betty's home. Missy went up and knocked on the front door.

Betty answered the door and missy curtsied to her and said good evening Miss. Betty let missy in, missy did not see any sign of Ken. Betty made missy spin around so she could get a full view of missy's dress. Betty gave missy a big smile and said better than I had hoped for, now let's discuss the rules and expectations so you can keep yourself out of trouble tonight, Betty said.

Betty told missy that all the snacks and drinks were on the bar next to the family room where everyone will be. Missy's job was to make sure everyone had all the drinks and snacks they wanted, very simple. When each lady arrives, missy was to introduce herself by saying, Hello, my name is maid missy and I am here to serve you, give them a nice curtsey, and show them to the family room and ask what you may serve them.

Betty told missy that she expects missy to never forget to be polite. Missy will answer any and all questions as you would for Miss T, no matter how embarrassing the questions may be. Missy could tell where that part was going. Missy was sure there would be many embarrassing questions for her.

Last, Betty said, I noticed that your dress is very short which is fine when you are standing up or walking. In fact with those fish net stockings and those 5 inch heels you have nicer legs then most of the girls on my team.

However, if you were to bend over you would clearly being showing off your panties. So remember this, missy, and be careful, no one will see you panties tonight unless I order them to be shown! You are to bend with your knees together as a lady server would do, as Miss T has taught you, do you understand me missy? Yes Miss Betty, I understand not to show off panties, as I curtsied to her.

That was great, Miss Betty said, about the curtsey thing. Do you always curtsey like that, missy? Yes Miss Betty, a maid always curtsies when she acknowledges an instruction, or as someone comes into the room or leaves or is introduced.

That's great Miss Betty said with a big smile, then make sure you do that too. So far Betty or should I say Miss Betty was not telling missy anything to do that she has not already been trained to do, so behavior should not be a problem for missy, missy thought.

Betty said, oh, one last thing, I had no plans to punish you tonight just for fun, so if you perform up to standards you may just serve us tonight without getting yourself into any trouble, but I expect complete obedience, do you understand? Yes Miss Betty, curtsey.

However, missy, if you disappoint me, I will not hesitate to punish you in front of my teammates. Yes Miss Betty, curtsey. OH, OH, I almost forgot something, Betty said. All of the ladies will be wearing tennis skirts or short tennis dresses, make sure you are not caught looking up their skirts at their panties! Yes Miss Betty, curtsey.

Missy's original concern was her own panties. Missy's dress is so short; not showing off missy's own panties is always a problem for missy. Missy will just have to be extremely careful on how she moves so she could handle that part of her panty problem.

However with those tennis skirts, some ladies don't seem to know how sit or move around while wearing those short skirts and dresses. So, the panty part could end up being a problem for me, missy thought, as it is just natural for me to look up the skirts of ladies when I had the chance.

I mean, ever since I was in grade school and the girls use to sit on the curb with their legs open and knees up giving the boys a good look between their legs at their panties.

Of course, I could never see anything other than the panties, but my point was that it was just a natural reaction to look in that area when a female gave me the opportunity to see her panties. So that night, I needed to be careful not to get missy in trouble.

Missy's second concern was because of the expected poor sitting position of some of the ladies as it could be difficult not having them think missy was looking even though missy was just facing their direction when they sat down, or crossed their legs or worse if they don't cross their legs. Missy thought that she would just have to make sure she looked away when there is any chance she could get a glance.

The Door bell sounded and missy went to answer it. Missy's first of several new humiliations that night missy thought. It is always much worse for missy when she met someone for the first time, especially dressed in her French maid outfit as she introduced herself as maid missy.

Anyway, missy answered the door to find a very tall blond lady standing there, she was maybe 6'0" tall, about 40 years old, sort of flat, with nice long shapely legs.

She had a nice ass and was better looking than average. Hello, my name is maid missy, welcome to Miss Betty's house, please come in, curtsey.

The Lady introduced herself as Cindy. It is nice to meet you Miss Cindy, curtsey. Miss Cindy followed missy to the family room, where missy asked her to please have a seat and asked what she may care to drink. Cindy told missy that she wanted a coke, yes Miss Cindy, curtsey.

Missy brought Miss Cindy a coke and made sure while placing it on the coffee table in front of Miss Cindy that missy had her side facing Miss Cindy so when missy stooped at the knees, with her knees together, like a playboy bunny is taught to serve, Miss Cindy would not be able to see missy's panties. Missy would need to make sure she kept that up all evening to make sure she does not show off her panties.

There was another knock at the door, missy excused herself from Miss Cindy, curtsied and went to answer the door. On the other side of the door was short lady, maybe 5'3" and somewhat stocky about 35 years old with medium length brown hair that just hung there and had no real style to it.

She was a very average looking 35 year old, with nothing special about her. Hello, I name is maid missy, welcome to Miss Betty's home, please come in, curtsey. Hi, she said, my name is Una. Yes, I know, I ever heard of that name either, but it is an old Scottish name, for real!

Miss Una, please follow me, curtsey. Like with Miss Cindy, missy showed Miss Una the way to the family room and got her a drink. As missy was delivering Miss Una's drink, Miss Betty came in and sat down.

Immediately, missy asked Miss Betty, is she could get her a drink, curtsey. Then there were three of them and apparently three more to come.

Apparently there are 6 members of the team. It seemed to missy that the ladies knew missy would be there serving them and knew missy was a sexy French maid as no one so far seemed surprised or even looked at missy funny. Rather they acted like they see sexy French maids all the time.

The three other ladies all came together. Nancy was about 5'8" about 40 years old, long brown hair and a very nice figure. Nancy was very pretty and had a nice smile. Missy guessed that in such a small town she should not have been surprised that Nancy was the same Miss Nancy from the dry cleaners. When Miss Nancy saw missy, she said OH! It's you missy, how nice.

The second lady was Tracy, who was also About 40 years old, 5"6", long blond hair, nice legs, sort of flat, but had a very nice ass and a great smile. Tracy also was very pretty.

Then there was Sue, About 25 years old, short black hair, about 5'10", nice long legs, decent size tits, and a very nice ass, she was also black and very pretty, with an outstanding smile. Betty, by the way is About 40 years old, 5'6", thin but with a nice figure, decent tits, nice ass, long blond hair and nice looking, also with a nice smile.

So far so good, missy got past the introductions and the first drink service without a missing a salutation, a curtsey, or showing off her panties. At the same time missy also managed to not get a look at any of the ladies panties.

However, I was finding that part extremely hard with what they were wearing and the way some of them sat. Let's be honest here, they are full grown middle aged women and missy knows how to sit without showing off her panties better than they do!

As missy continued to refill drinks and snack bowls, Miss Betty asked missy, you know missy, you have very nice legs, thank you Miss Betty, curtsey. You also curtsey very nicely, how long have you been a maid

who curtsies like that? I have been trained
as a maid by my mother and sister since I
was about 13 and I have been serving Miss T
for almost two months.

Miss Sue, jumped in with, I understand
that Miss T spanks and punishes you in other
ways if you don't behave, is that all true,
missy? Yes Miss Sue, curtsey.

I also understand that Betty got to give
you get a spanking a week or so ago, is that
right missy, asked Miss Cindy? Yes Miss
Cindy, curtsey. Miss Cindy continued; and
that was with a solid wood hairbrush, missy?
Yes, Miss Cindy, curtsey. Wow! that must
have really hurt. Yes Miss Cindy, curtsey.

Miss Betty interrupted missy's humiliation
to have drinks and snacks replenished, but
missy knew they were not finished with her
yet as they were having too much fun and some
of them did not have to courage to start on
missy yet, yet missy was sure that would
change as the night moved on.

As missy was back to serving she could
hear comments that the ladies were making
as they discussed tennis, men, other women,
and they discussed missy. They seemed to
agree that missy looked pretty good in her
maid uniform, had nice legs, a trim waist,
a nice smile, and a nice ass.

Miss Betty started to tell them about missy's ass and how nice it really was and how excited she got while she was spanking it.

Miss Betty told them that she always gets excited when spanking Ken and that he always satisfies her afterwards with a good pussy licking. Miss Betty told them that after spanking missy her pussy was soaking wet and when she got home she had Ken lick her to four orgasms in only 15 minutes.

Well, missy guessed that everyone already knew that Miss Betty spanked her boyfriend, Ken, and now missy also knows. Missy thought that explained Miss T's instructions to Ken that he was not to feel sorry for missy when he gave her that strapping or he would be sorry. Miss T obviously knew that Ken was submissive to Miss Betty and would be punished if he failed to satisfy Miss T

After everything was refilled, Miss Betty had missy stand with her back to the window so she was facing everyone and the questioning and the humiliation continued.

By the way, before we go any further, did anybody notice that the first initial of each of the five ladies names, without Miss Betty, spelled out "C.U.N.T.S." Miss Cindy, Miss Una, Miss Nancy, Miss Tracy, and Miss Sue. What are the chances? So, now missy knows two sets of ladies, the

B.I.T.C.H.S and the C.U.N.T.S. Again, what are the chances of that happing?

Anyway, Miss Betty told missy to turn around and lower her panties and show all the ladies her well spanked ass, yes Miss, curtsey. Missy could feel the blood flush to her face as her embarrassment level shot up. However, missy had no choice in the matter unless she wanted to show the girls a real spanking for being disobedient.

As missy turned around, she lowered her panties and lifted up the back of her short dress to show all the C.U.N.T.S. her ass that was still pretty black and blue from the spanking that Miss Betty gave her 9 days ago.

Most of the ladies did comment on how nice an ass missy had. While others also added that Miss Betty must know how to give a hell of a spanking that would still show so much black and blue after 9 days. That part was sure true, Miss Betty knew how to give a hell of a spanking, missy thought.

Alright missy, Miss Betty said; pull up your panties and turn around. Missy pulled up her panties and turned around and said yes Miss and curtseyed to Miss Betty as was ready for more humiliation.

Miss Una was the first to go that time. Missy, is it true that part of your maid duties would be to eat my cunt if I wanted you to? Miss Una is the chunky one of the group; sort of the black sheep of the team as far as looks are concerned.

Miss Una was not married, so missy guessed she would be the one to ask such a question as she would be the one in most need. Especially with that mouth, she must not get much male attention. No Miss Una, sexual services can only be granted by Miss T, curtsey.

Miss Nancy said; missy, I noticed you shave your legs; I noticed that before in your tennis shorts, but now I know why. Do you shave the rest of your body as well, yes Miss Nancy, I am completely shaven, curtsey.

Well, I guess that answered my question about if the ladies knew that I was also Jack and if they knew I was really a guy. I guess Miss T told them everything. Nevertheless, they seemed fine with me being a sexy French maid for them as no one seemed to complain that I was a guy at a girls party.

Miss Tracy said missy; tell us about the spanking that you got from Betty, you know verbally walk us through the whole spanking thing from the beginning to the end. Yes Miss, curtsey.

So, to humiliate herself even more, missy had to give them all the details about how the Miss Betty spanking turned out. Including the corner time before and after the spanking.

Miss Una spoke up again; I want to get back to this sex thing, are you telling me missy that if we got your Miss T's permission that you would have to eat all 6 of our cunts, if that's what we wanted you to do? Yes Miss Una, curtsey.

Miss Sue spoke up, Tell us missy, have you been punished with other instruments beside a hairbrush? Yes Miss Sue, I have been punished with a cane, a strap, and with a wood paddle, curtsey.

Tell us, which one is worse missy. The cane is the worst followed by the strap and then the wood hairbrush. Miss Sue told missy to tell them how the brush, the strap and cane were different, yes miss, curtsey.

Missy explained that the cane stings at first very badly and then starts to burn more and more as the seconds pass as the sting goes deep down into the muscle. As there are more and more cane welts delivered, there are more areas to burn so the pain multiplies more then with a strap or hairbrush.

The strap hurts the most on impact, but does not have a pain building part like the

cane does. Once you get past the initial
impact of the strap, the pain starts to
decrease.

The hairbrush hurts a lot on impact but
only covers a small area and the pain, like
the strap starts to decrease over time.
However, with the hairbrush someone can take
many more strokes of the brush, so a spanking
can be more intense as in more strokes per
minute and can last a much longer time Miss
sue, curtsey.

So, missy, why do you get spanked more
often than the cane or the strap? Missy
told Miss Sue, I suppose that a hairbrush
spanking is simply sufficient and it's more
humiliating being spanked like a kid over a
ladies knees, curtsey.

Miss Sue, it may also be that the lady
just enjoys giving me the spanking. Keeping
in mind that I am punished to remind me to
obey better in the future and not to be
cruel, a spanking is usually enough to gain
my cooperation so why should she be more
severe then she needs to be.

Additionally, Miss Sue, if I was always
caned, there would be no worse punishment
available if I was extra bad, curtsey. One
more question, you did not mention a whip,
have you never been whipped? No Miss sue,
curtsey.

I don't know about the rest of you, but I am totally enjoying this evening, much more than I thought I would, said Miss Betty. I just love the way missy looks and answers our questions and has to curtsey all the time, and everyone clapped in agreement.

Well, said Miss Sue; I could not agree more, however I would love to be the first one to whip missy, I would just love to take her outback, tie her up to a tree and give her a good whipping. I would love to whip that maid, just like an old time slave would get a whipping from their mistress. YEA, that did not sound like a good idea! Missy thought.

Back to Miss Una, Tell me missy, do you like eating cunt? Would you just have a great time eating all of us? Una has such a way with words and that seemed to be all that was on her mind, her cunt, missy thought.

Miss Una, I have little experience with such tasks. I have only satisfied Miss T and Miss Beth in that way so far. However, I did enjoy pleasing Miss T and Miss Beth as well. So, yes I do look forward to pleasing Miss T and Miss Beth in that way in the future, curtsey.

Miss Betty took a turn; missy do you enjoy being a maid? Yes Miss, curtsey. Miss Betty continued; do you like being humiliated like

we are doing to you now just for our own
fun? No Miss Betty, curtsey.

Do you enjoy being punished? No Miss,
curtsey. Then, missy, why do you accept the
humiliation and the punishment.

Missy told the ladies, that she was not
totally sure and all she could tell them was
that it is all part of being a sissy maid
and being submissive to a dominate women
and she enjoys those parts so that she needs
to accept the parts she does not enjoy as
well.

After all, ladies, I would not get punished
if I was more obedient, so any punishments I
do receive are all my own fault, curtsey.

Missy told the ladies that Miss T and her
mother have both told her that in the long
run that she will be happier in life if she
simply obeys the women in her life, so she
does and it seems to be working as overall
she is very happy, Miss, curtsey.

I have a Different kind of question for
missy, Miss Una said. Do you know if your
Miss T has given permission to Betty for
any of us to be able to get you to eat out
our cunts tonight? No Miss Una, I do not,
Curtsey.

Then, missy, how would you know if it
was alright if we just told you to eat us?

Miss Una, I can only trust Miss Betty not
to allow anything unauthorized by Miss T as
Miss T trusts Miss Betty or she would not
have allowed me to come over tonight, Miss,
curtsey.

   Miss Una continued; she just would not
let it go, missy thought! Missy, would the
same be true for spanking you? Yes Miss Una,
only Miss Betty knows what Miss T as agreed
to permit for tonight, Miss Una, curtsey.

   So really what you are saying, missy, is
that when you came here tonight, you had no
idea and still don't as to what the scope
of our authority over you for tonight might
be, is that correct? Yes, Miss Una, that is
correct, only Miss Betty and anybody she
would tell would know, Miss, curtsey.

   Missy thought that Miss Una had her mind
set on missy licking her pussy for her and
she was going to do or say or ask anything
she had to, to get missy to do it. However,
missy was hoping she did not need to lick
Miss Una's pussy as she was so unattractive
and had such a filthy mouth. Miss Una was
so un-lady like and missy really wanted
nothing to do with her.

   Miss Tracy took a turn at humiliating
missy; missy is it true that you have been
spanked over your own sisters knees, by your
sister? Yes Miss, curtsey. Missy, did you

find that to be more humiliating than when
your Mom spanked you? Yes Miss, Curtsey.

Missy is it also true that your sister
has spanked you in front of one of her
girlfriends as well? Yes Miss, curtsey.
Missy did you sister also spank you in front
of your own girlfriend and her boyfriend
and make you stand in the corner in front of
them as well? Yes, Miss, curtsey.

Missy, was there anything that you found
more humiliating then that spanking and that
corner time? No miss, curtsey.

Miss Una finally asked a question not
related to getting her pussy attended to,
she asked; missy do you think that being
obedient and submissive provides some sort
of sexual satisfaction to you? Yes Miss,
curtsey.

So if your Miss T makes you eat her out
every single day for a month that's ok
with you missy, Miss Una asked? Yes Miss,
curtsey

Well, Miss Una continued; all I know is
that I need to get myself a sissy maid of my
own, this sounds too good to be true! Miss
Una continued; if I can get my pussy tended
to all I want and don't need to worry about
the guys satisfaction, and I can get my house
cleaned, and I can get total obedience, and

I can even punish her if I'm unhappy in any way, Sign me up!

Miss Una stood up and said the she had a great time but if she is not getting her cunt eaten then it's time to be going. Missy's heart started pounding little harder as she did not know if Miss Betty had permission to tell missy to eat Miss Una's pussy, or not.

But, missy did think that if she had to lick Miss Una's pussy, most likely she would need to service all 6 pussies, not something missy was looking forward to doing. Missy did enjoy licking Miss T and Miss Beth's pussy's, however, missy like both Miss T and Miss Beth. These ladies were just strangers, not the same thing missy thought.

Miss Betty looked at missy and gave her a big smile, almost like saying yes Miss Una could have her wish, but then turned to Miss Una and told her that Miss T did not provide such authorization.

This was a huge relief for missy. Missy did not think Miss T would have given Miss Betty such permission, and missy would have bet 10 to 1 against it. But, on the other hand, missy would have bet 4 or 5 to 1 against Miss T agreeing for missy to be there at all that evening.

One thing about Miss T, you just never know for sure what she will or not make missy do. Miss T was unpredictable and Miss T likes it that way. Missy finds that un-nerving to a degree. However, so far, Miss T has not been cruel or overly punishing of missy, or has done anything else that would make missy want not to be her sissy maid.

Oh Well, said Miss Una, I'll be going now and stood up to say goodbye, as Miss Cindy said how about a spanking? Miss Betty looked at her and said, Cindy, you want a spanking? No silly, I would like to see missy get a spanking, I have never seen such a thing and think it would be a fun experience to see missy get a spanking.

Miss Nancy then said that missy had behaved very well for us. Missy, has been perfectly polite, served us well, and answered all of our questions honestly. Don't you think that missy needs to do something wrong to get a spanking? Miss Nancy questioned.

Ladies, Miss Betty continued; should we decide to spank missy just for our own fun? Missy was getting nervous that she was going to get a spanking in front of all the C.U.N.T.S. just for their own fun, but really, just because Miss Una did not get her pussy licked and she was finding a reason to get missy punished for it, even though to lick or not to lick Miss Una's pussy was simply was not up to missy anyway.

Miss Una then said that she thinks missy needs to be punished for looking up her dress and looking at her panties all evening. Missy knew that Miss Una was lying as Miss Una's panties would be the last set of panties in that room that she wanted to see.

Miss Una did not know that her lies were reason enough for missy to get a spanking, rather Miss Una was just shooting in the dark, hoping for the best. Miss Una was just a first class bitch, missy thought.

Miss Betty thought about it for a minute and then told missy to go and get one of the kitchen chairs and bring it in here and place it there in front of the window, yes Miss, curtsey.

Missy was not happy and missy was very disappointed to find out that Miss Betty did find that Miss Una's lies were enough for Miss Betty to decide to give missy a spanking.

Missy really wanted to object as Miss Una was lying, but it was missy's word against Miss Una and since the flavor of the room was looking for an excuse to spank missy, missy was not about to do or say anything that would embarrass Miss T as then she would truly be punished by Miss T when she got home. Being Miss T's maid could be a hard task sometimes missy thought.

Missy nevertheless obeyed Miss Betty as Miss Betty left the room. Missy assumed that she was going to get the spanking brush. Missy brought the chair back and placed it in front of the window so that the other five ladies could all get a clear view.

Miss Betty did come back with a spanking brush that was very similar in size to Miss T's. As soon as missy saw the hairbrush in Miss Betty hand, missy's embarrassment started to kick in big time as missy's face started to get red hot and worse, missy's cock started to grow again.

Miss Betty sat down the chair and being somewhat of a Miss T of humiliation herself; Miss Betty told missy to go over to Miss Tracy and ask her to remove your panties for your spanking. How did missy know that Miss Betty would take a very humiliating situation and make it even worse for missy? Yes Miss, curtsey.

Missy walked slowly over to Miss Tracy. As missy did she could feel her cock still growing almost too full size at that point? Miss Tracy, would you please remove my panties for my spanking, missy asked, every quietly, curtsey.

Immediately, Miss Betty spoke up and said missy, we all did not hear you, speak louder! Missy turned around to face Miss Betty, yes Miss, curtsey. Missy started anew and asked

Miss Tracy again, only louder, Miss Tracy, would you please remove my panties so Miss Betty can spank me, curtsey?

Miss Tracy said of course I will, as she put her hands up under missy's very short dress and petticoat and slipped missy's panties down to her knees. Is that far enough missy, Miss Tracy asked? Yes Miss, curtsey.

As missy walked back to Miss Betty, Miss Cindy said, wait a minute, what's that pushing the front of missy's dress out? Miss Una stuck her hand out and pulled up the front of missy's dress to see, as everyone saw missy's erection.

Look at that said Miss Sue, missy's penis thinks this is a good idea too, and they all laughed at missy, intensifying missy's humiliation. Miss Una let go of missy's dress and missy continued to walk over to Miss Betty. Miss Betty said to them; don't worry about that I'll spank that erection off missy in a minute.

Miss Betty looked at missy and asked, are you ready for your spanking missy? Yes Miss, curtsey. Missy was ever so worried that Miss Betty would give her a long hard spanking and since the spanking was only for the C.U.N.T.S. fun, or so missy thought, missy thought that she should only get a short simple spanking, you know one that does not hurt so much and does not last as long as a real punishments spanking. At least missy was hoping that Miss Betty knew that Miss Una was lying and would take it easy on her.

Miss Betty told missy to lay over her lap, yes Miss, curtsey. Missy laid over Miss Betty's lap as she felt her cock dig into Miss Betty's left thigh and waited for the spanking to begin.

Missy felt totally humiliated being in the spanking position in front of all the C.U.N.T.S.; not only because missy was about to be spanked like a little girl, but because they all play tennis at the same club. So, missy could only assume that they will tell others in the club thereby extending missy's humiliation indefinitely.

Miss Betty lifted missy's dress up and folded it over onto her back. Missy heard one of the ladies say, missy really does have a nice ass; the first spank landed with a loud crack.

Miss Betty continued the spanking one spank about every two seconds and reasonably hard. In spite of missy's desire not to make much of a fuss to humiliate herself further in front of the ladies, spankings do hurt and they hurt a lot, so it was not too long before missy was kicking her legs and OUCH, OH, OUCH, OH, OH, OUCH!

Miss Betty continued to; SPANK missy and SPANK missy and SPANK missy and SPANK missy, on and on and on. By the time Miss Betty reached 25 or 30 spanks, missy's whimpering intensified and missy's crying started a little also.

By the time missy received 50 spanks she had kicked her panties off, was whimpering a lot, and crying more steadily. Miss Betty continued to spank missy the same way until Miss Betty delivered about 100 spanks and missy was crying steadily, but not heavily.

Miss Beth stopped spanking missy and told her that she could get up. Missy was happy that Miss Betty did not give her a long hard spanking like Miss T does. Missy got right up and stood to Miss Betty's side and said thank you Miss for my spanking, I am sorry I was naughty. Missy was hoping that that would make everyone happy and that would be the end of her "Show" for the evening.

Miss Betty told missy that she could go and find her panties and put them back on, yes Miss, curtsey. All the C.U.N.T.S. started clapping and telling Miss Betty that she did a great job spanking missy and they thought it was a great time.

As missy walked past Miss Una to fetch her panties, Miss Una stopped her and put her hand back up under missy's dress to check to see if Miss Betty really did spank the erection off of missy and found out that Miss Betty actually did.

It took about 10 minutes for everyone to say their goodbyes. As missy was cleaning up; she heard a lot of comments about much fun they had that evening and can they do it again sometime and especially how much they enjoyed seeing missy spanked.

After the last one was out the door, Miss Betty told missy to put everything away or in the dish washer. Yes Miss, curtsey. Missy was thinking about whether or not miss T was going to punish her further when she got home as Miss T usually does add additional corner time to all of missy's punishments?

Missy was hoping that because she really did not do anything wrong, as that spanking was really an entertainment spanking, that Miss T would not be annoyed with her or disappointed in her. However, I noticed that missy's main focus was on not disappointing Miss T and not being concerned about standing in the corner.

Missy cleaned everything; Miss Betty inspected, approved, and gave missy permission to leave. Miss Betty did tell missy, as she walked her to the front door, that she knew Una was lying and that was why she only gave missy a token spanking. Thank you Miss Betty, curtsey.

MO MISS T PUSSY:

When missy got home that Saturday night, she found a note on her front door to report to Miss T. Missy went downstairs to Miss T's room and said Miss T you wished to see me, curtsey?

Yes missy, come on in and tell me about your evening. Missy told Miss T everything and Miss T told missy that she knew the girls were going to find a reason to give you a moderate spanking. So as it turned out Miss T gave them permission to spank missy but she would not let missy lick any of their pussies.

So missy, did you enjoy yourself over all, not considering the spanking? Miss T, may I ask you a question before I answer you? Alright Missy, go ahead. Thank you Miss, curtsey. My question is, Miss T, did you enjoy that I went there to entertain your friends? Was my obedience pleasing and exciting to you Miss?

That's an interesting question that you are asking missy, the answer is definitely yes. Then, Miss T, I also had a good time. Miss T asked missy to expound upon her answer, yes miss, curtsey.

Missy told Miss T that for her to go to some stranger's home and to be spanked and humiliated all night for their pleasure was not particularly satisfying for her. Missy said that she would have been happier to stay home and continue cleaning the house for Miss T.

However, if I was going there to be spanked and humiliated to please you, Miss T, then I was happy to do it. Miss T if I made you happy and I had the feeling that I was pleasing you it made the night worthwhile for me too. Missy, with a tear in her eye continued to say, after all Miss T, you are the one I wish to please, not them Miss, curtsey.

Well missy, Miss T said, I appreciate your thoughts as they mean a lot to me and the truth is that just thinking about what was going on over there has had me excited all night to the point where my pussy has been wet for hours.

So I think the best thing for you to do missy, is to get up here on the bed and slid you face up here, as Miss T opened her robe, between my legs and lick me real good. Missy smiled, yes Miss, curtsey, as missy was happy to lick Miss T's pussy for her.

Licking pussy was still very new to missy, but she seemed to have a good time the last time with Miss T. And, as missy told Miss T that evening, missy was finding her own pleasure in obeying Miss T.

Missy was rock hard before she even got her face close enough to touch Miss T's pussy with her lips. However, missy knew that would not matter to Miss T as she was not there to cum, missy was there to make Miss T cum and missy was going to make sure she did the best she could to please Miss T and make Miss T happy.

Missy started out just like Miss T told her to last time and used her lips and tongue on the inside of Miss T's thighs and slowly licked up and down the inside of her thighs just below Miss T's beautiful pussy lips as Miss T moaned just a bit.

Missy did the same on Miss T's other thigh and Miss T wiggled a bit for her. Then missy started to kiss Miss T real gently all along the inside of Miss T's thighs alternating between the right and the left, the left and the right.

Slowly missy moved her mouth up towards Miss T's pussy and started to kiss and lick the outside of Miss T's pussy lips, first the

right side and then the left side, kissing
and licking and licking and gently licking
and kissing while missy moved her hands up
under Miss T great ass and started squeezing
Miss T's ass cheek ever so gently.

Missy moved to the front and inside of
Miss T's pussy lips and began kissing and
licking and licking and kissing both the
front and the inside of each lip while at
the same time she would use her hands to
adjust the pressure against her mouth by
squeezing tighter or relaxing her hands.

Missy started to lick Miss T's pussy
lips a little stronger and licked from the
bottom to the top like an ice cream cone
and pulled Miss T tighter to missy's tongue
with her arms. That got more of a reaction
out of Miss T as Miss T started to squirm
more, moan more and even moved her hips
involuntary.

Missy kept that up for a minute or so and
she kept going deeper and deeper with her
tongue with each lick until she could not
get her tongue inside of Miss T's pussy any
deeper.

Missy pulled Miss T even closer with her
arms thereby pushing her entire face into
Miss T's pussy and licked Miss T a bit more
while moving her head back and forth back
and forth.

Missy started to lick around Miss T's clit but did not touch it yet. Missy thought she was exciting Miss T and at the same time frustrating Miss T. Then Miss T yelled out, NOW missy! NOW missy!

Missy immediately started licking her tongue all over Miss T's clit and Miss T exploded all over missy's face in wave after wave after wave of orgasmic delight.

Finally Miss T just nudged missy's head with her hand and missy knew that Miss T needed a break. Missy laid her head on the inside of Miss T's thigh and just stayed there with Miss T until Miss T was ready to move. Miss T sighed and breathed heavy and then said, Oh missy! Oh missy! That was great!

A couple of minutes later Miss T tapped missy on the head which missy took as a signal that Miss T was ready for another round and missy went right back to work. That time missy was a little more aggressive from the start and had Miss T moaning much louder that time and had Miss T wiggling much more that time and missy even had Miss T bucking her hips more this time.

In less than two minutes as missy pulled Miss T real tight by pulling up on her ass cheeks and smashing her face in to Miss T's pussy and Miss T started another wave after wave of orgasmic delight.

Once more when Miss T was finished she pushed missy's head away very gently and missy again rested her head on the inside of Miss T's thigh waiting to find out if Miss T wanted another or if Miss T was finished. Miss T tapped missy on the head and again missy went back to work for the third time and again for a fourth time before Miss T was finished.

Alright Miss T said, that was great, just great, I'm finished now, clean me, yes Miss and missy went to work licking up all of the juices she could with her tongue. Miss T told missy to move over while Miss T turned over.

Miss T placed a pillow under her hips and told missy to clean her ass was well, yes Miss. Missy licked and kissed and sucked on Miss T's beautiful ass cheeks even though there was no pussy juices on them. Missy was just having a good time as she was discovering that she really liked licking and sucking on Miss T's fine ass.

Then missy started to lick all the juices out of Miss T's crack and again missy was lingering enjoying herself. Miss T noticed and told missy to finish up and missy dove into Miss T's crack with her tongue and cleaned Miss T's ass hole.

Missy had a nice time pleasing Miss T that evening. Additionally, when missy was leaving for the evening, Miss T gave missy permission to masturbate that evening and missy did so twice before she got undressed so that I could go to sleep.

LATER:

About a week later, Miss Sue, the black lady with the nice body saw me at the tennis club. She was playing with Miss Cindy and she waved to me to come over to her court. I had no idea what she may have wanted, but I would not take the chance to ignore her and possibly get myself into trouble.

I walked over to Miss Sue and said good afternoon Miss Sue, how may I help you? Miss Sue said; I just wanted to tell you that we had a great time the other night, even if it was at your expense and we all knew that Una was lying as no one looks at her, she's a pig, however, she is a good tennis player.

I thanked Miss Sue for her comments and told her to have a nice day. As I walked away, I started to think again if they would be telling all of their friends about me being missy also.

I assumed with the little I knew about women, that they surely would tell all of their friend over time. Accordingly, over time everyone in the tennis club would know all about me and missy.

That thought did not make me feel all that good, but I guessed I would see how it played out. I really did not want to stop playing tennis and it was the only tennis club in that small town.

THE DOOR BELL, RERUN:

As I have told you, missy was always worried about embarrassing herself when she had to answer the front door. Miss T did not make missy answer the front door until enough time went by so that missy was finished being trained well enough so that she looked like and acted like a real female French maid. After that time, the front door was missy's responsibility to answer.

One morning, missy had to answer the front door when the bell rang around 10 am. All the girls were all at school and missy was home alone. Missy heard the door bell and felt a shot of nervous tension thru her tummy. Keep in mind that missy does not know who is on the other side of the door when she answered it.

Missy went to the front door and with her hand shaking a little bit opened the door and said, good morning, my name is maid missy, how I may help you, curtsey.

Missy did not think that answering the door was not really as bad a curtseying in the dry cleaners of even on the sidewalk that time when Miss T was sitting on the bench, but he was still a stranger and it was very embarrassing, especially after missy got the smile she got from him.

The guy was a very nice looking blond headed man about 35 years old with a very nice smile. He was about 6'2" and looked like he had a nice body. He was the TV repairman as two TV's were not getting proper reception. This was the second time the TV man had to come to fix the reception for some of the TV's, however, this was a different repair man.

The man introduced himself and said that he needed to see the two TV's and then he may have to adjust the antenna on the roof. Missy told the guy to follow her and she was very aware that she looked great from the back and that if she was him, she would be thinking about how nice it would be to fuck the maid. Especially as missy takes her very small ass wiggling female steps as she walked along in front of the man.

Missy led the man up to the second floor and showed him the two TV's in Miss Heather's room and in Miss Ida's room. He check them out and told me that he would be back and went up on the roof and adjusted the antenna for those two TV's and he came back and they were both fine.

We went back downstairs and missy asked him if he would care for a cold drink and he gave missy a big smile and said no think you and started to leave, but then turned around and asked missy if she always curtsies like that or was he just special as he smiled at her again as if to flirt with missy.

Yes, Sir, I always curtsey to everyone. And, missy, just why do you curtsey like that if you do not mind me asking? Sir, Miss T, my employer requires me to curtsey. Oh really, he said; Do you always do everything your so called Miss T tells you to do? Yes Sir, curtsey. Interesting, he said; as he walked down the path to his truck and left.

BETH'S WONDERFUL PUSSY:

Miss T told missy that she wanted to see her that evening after missy had finished all her chores for the day. Missy had no idea what was on Miss T's mind, however Miss T sure did not seem upset with missy and missy knew that she had been very well behaved.

Missy thought that maybe she forgot to do something, but then, she figured that Miss T would not wait until later in the evening and punish her privately in Miss T's room if that was the case.

So then, Missy thought that perhaps that Miss T wanted missy to lick her ass or even lick her pussy for her or both. Missy was all up for that idea, literally.

I mean as missy was just thinking that perhaps that was why Miss T wanted her, missy got a rock hard erection that did not go away for almost 30 minutes.

Missy reported to Miss T's room around 9:30 pm and knocked on her door frame and said; good evening Miss T, you wished to see me, curtsey.

Yes Missy, come on in. Thank you, miss, curtsey. Missy went into Miss T's room and Miss T spoke quietly to missy so no one else could hear. Missy, I had been speaking with Miss Beth.

Miss Beth tells me that you have pleased her ass and have pleased her pussy for her like you have please mine. However, missy, I did not know that until tonight. Anyway, missy, you can continue to please Miss Beth whenever she wishes you to, however, do not take such instructions from anyone else without my permission first.

Missy, I don't want you to worry about having to provide sexual service to anyone and everyone upon their command. That was why I did not give Miss Betty permission for you to service her tennis friends.

So, in the future, missy, you are free to tell anyone else that I do not permit you to do such things without anyone without my permission in advance and I will not consider your refusal to please them as disobedience on your part. Alright missy? Yes Miss, thank you, curtsey.

Alright missy, you can go and see Miss Beth now as she is waiting for you. Thank you, Miss, curtsey.

Missy turned around and went down and across the hallway to Miss Beth's room. Missy knocked on the door frame and said; good evening Miss Beth, you wished to see me, curtsey.

Yes missy come on in as Miss Beth wiggled high up on her bed with her head on a pillow near the headboard. Miss Beth flipped the bed covers off of her and missy got to enjoy the sight of Miss Beth's beautiful body. DAMN, missy thought Miss Beth had a great body, so well-proportioned and muscled toned.

Missy right away looked at Miss Beth's pussy area and found what missy thought was a very nice triangle of fur between Beth's very nice thighs. Missy got an instant erection and was sure hoping that she could use her erection to please herself, however, missy knew that was not in the cards as Miss Beth only wanted to use missy's tongue between those great looking thighs of hers.

Miss Beth did not say anything, rather she just pointed towards her pussy and missy got on the bed and crawled up between Miss Beth's legs. As missy approached Miss Beth's pussy with her mouth, Miss Beth spread her legs a little to give missy more room.

Miss Beth seemed to be very shy and very excited. Missy understood that Miss Beth had never had someone with their face and lips and tongue between her legs before other than that first time with missy, so Miss Beth was still somewhat nervous.

At the same time, missy could smell the aroma of an excited pussy. It smelled completely different than Miss T's pussy, but it did not smell bad to missy. Rather just a scent that missy did not like and did not object too, all at the same time.

Missy moved her face down to Miss Beth's pussy area and started to just use just her lips, kissing gently on the inside of Miss Beth's thighs and then slowly used her tongue to lick up and down on the inside of Miss Beth's very nice thighs to just below her beautiful pussy lips.

That did not get a reaction from Miss Beth, however missy did not know if it was because Miss Beth did not really like it or if Miss Beth was still too nervous to enjoy herself.

So, missy started to kiss Miss Beth again but more strongly all along the inside of Miss Beth's thighs alternating between the right thigh and the left thigh, the left thigh and the right thigh. That got a little wiggle and a little moan of pleasure from Miss Beth.

Missy moved her mouth up towards Miss Beth's pussy and started to gently kiss Miss Beth's pussy lips. Miss Beth really liked that and started moaning much louder and flopping her head around and making other sounds as well.

Missy moved on and started to lick the outside of Miss Beth's pussy lips, first the right side and then the left side, kissing and licking and kissing and gently licking and kissing some more.

Miss Beth started to squirm a lot more and Miss Beth moaned a lot more and Miss Beth even shivered a little. Miss Beth was flopping her head back and forth and told missy that is great, missy, just great, your lips and tongue feel so good!!!!!!!!! MISSY!

Missy moved my lips to the front of Miss Beth's pussy and put her tongue on the inside of Miss Beth's pussy and began kissing and licking and licking and kissing both the front and the inside of each of Miss Beth's soft and delicious pussy lips.

Miss Beth was squirming and moaning even more. Missy started to lick Miss Beth's pussy lips a little stronger and licked from the bottom to the top of one of Miss Beth pussy lips and then on the other side over and over and over again and Miss Beth seemed like she could not be any more pleased or excited. Miss Beth started to squirm more, moan more and even moved her hips seemingly involuntary.

Missy kept that up for a minute or so as missy kept going deeper and deeper with into Miss Beth's pussy with her tongue, deeper with each lick until missy could not get my tongue inside of Miss Beth's pussy any deeper.

Missy started to lick around Miss Beth's clit. However, apparently Miss Beth could not take missy teasing her any longer as Miss Beth started saying NOW MISSY! NOW! DO IT NOW, MISSY!

Missy started licking her tongue all over Miss Beth's clit and Miss Beth exploded all over missy's face in wave after wave after wave of orgasmic delight.

When Beth was finished cuming she sort of jerked her hips away from missy and missy laid her head down on the inside of Miss Beth's thigh just like she did with Miss T.

About three or five minutes later Miss Beth whispered, AGAIN MISSY AGAIN! Missy smiled to herself and was happy to give Miss Beth another good long licking. Missy was realizing that she enjoyed pleasing Miss Beth even more then she enjoyed pleasing Miss T.

Missy thought that had to be because she always had some sort of attraction to Miss Beth as they had known one another for years and were friends.

Missy went right back to work, this time she was a little more aggressive from the start and had Miss Beth moaning much louder than before and had Miss Beth wiggling much more than before and even had Miss Beth bucking her hips more than before. In less than two minutes missy was smashing her face into Miss Beth's pussy and Miss Beth started another wave after wave after wave of orgasmic delight.

Once more when Miss Beth was finished she jerked her hips away from missy's mouth and missy very gently rested her head on the inside of Miss Beth's thigh waiting to find out if Miss Beth wanted another or if Miss Beth was finished.

A few minutes later Miss Beth signaled missy again and missy was ever so happy to give Miss Beth the pussy licking of her life. Missy was really enjoying having her face in Miss Beth's pussy and making Miss Beth wiggle all over the bed.

Before the night was over missy had made Miss Beth cum four times and everyone seemed more explosive than the one before.

When Miss Beth finally had enough, missy went to the bathroom and came back with a nice hot towel and cleaned all around Miss Beth's dripping wet pussy.

Missy asked Miss Beth to turn over and missy also cleaned all around Miss Beth's ass crack and anus for her as well. Last, missy leaned over and gave Miss Beth's ass cheeks a few very gentle kisses.

Miss Beth thanked missy and told her she was dismissed. However, missy was hoping that missy Beth was going to give missy permission to masturbate that evening, but, Miss Beth did not.

Good night Miss, curtsey, and missy left.

SUMMARY:

Well, I have given you the highlights of my first two months of collage as well as my first two months as a sissy maid to seven college girls.

I have discovered so far that missy not only does not mind doing most of the housework, rather missy actually enjoys serving the seven ladies, or B.I.T.C.H.S.

However, they were not really bitches at all. Miss T had been great teaching missy what to do, teaching missy how to look and act like a lady, and punishing missy fairly when she was disobedient. Missy really liked and respected Miss T.

Missy also discovered that she liked to have her face in Miss T' ass as well as Miss Beth's ass. I had never done anything like that before, but missy enjoyed it and missy expects to be able to enjoy it a lot more in the future as both Miss T and Miss Beth liked it as well.

Next, Miss T taught missy how to please a pussy with missy's mouth and tongue and missy loved that even more than licking their asses for them. As well, Miss T and Miss Beth both seemed to really enjoy having missy lick their pussy's a whole lot. So, missy was expecting to be able to continue to enjoy that pleasure going forward as well.

Missy found out that the hardest part of her sissy maid job was to go out in public and embarrass and humiliate herself to no end at the dry cleaners and at home when answering the front door.

Missy would have been happier if she could just stay in the house and be the sissy maid there all the time. Nevertheless, missy understood that she had no choice in the matter as Miss T decided what missy would do and what missy would not do.

Missy did not think that avoiding that embarrassment and or humiliation was worth the price of going and living in the dorm with a bunch of guys. Besides, at that point in time, missy would really miss, Miss T and Miss Beth.

Missy could also do without the punishments. However, missy also understood as her mother taught her real well, that she can avoid punishments by behaving properly and being obedient to the women in her life.

Once again, missy did not think avoiding punishment was a good reason to leave the house and go to live in the dorm.

Missy had an interesting experience with Mom and Miss Jill as they went out to dinner and missy was cross dressed as a sexy girl. Missy found that experience to be very exciting and had fantasized about such cross dressed for many years. Missy would also look forward to doing that again as well.

So, how am I doing? I am doing very well in college and am getting good test marks and have not found it to be very difficult at all.

I have not had that much time to play baseball or tennis as missy was so busy with her cleaning and other tasks.

I have not had any time to date for the same reasons, not a lot of free time. However, missy has made up for some of it with her growing relationship with Miss T and Miss Beth and their respective asses and pussy's.

Overall, what does missy and I feel about being the sissy maid to the house for seven girls? So far, both missy and I are very happy with the deal.

THE SISSY MAID MISSY SERIES OF BOOKS

by M MISSY

First there was the Sissy Maid Missy series that covered the life of a sissy maid from his/her growing years in the;

SPANKING DIARY,
and

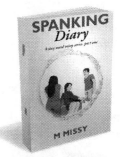

SPANKINGS, AND SUBMISSION TO MY WIFE

Missy discovered the great internal desire to be a sissy maid to his/her wife, who caused may problems in their relationship.

Those problems concluded with Missy going to live with Mistress in;

A SISSY MAIDS LIFE,

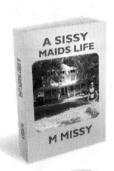

A SISSY MAIDS LIFE,
Two

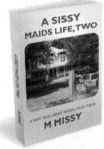

A SISSY MAIDS LIFE,
Three

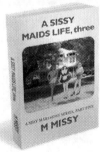

As a full time Sissy Maid for Mistress's large home. Missy's life moved along. Later Missy tried to reunite with her wife and that story is still developing.

The Sissy Maid Life series includes Female domination, male submission, spankings, canings, strappings, whippings, sexual submission to both sexes, bondage, corner time, cross dressing, and humiliation of the sissy maid.

The second series begins with;

SISTER, SPANKINGS, SISSY MAID

This is the story of Twin children, one boy and one girl, and how they were raised back in the 50's and 60's by their mother. It includes spankings, hairbrush spankings, a strapping, witness humiliation, corner time, nudity, femdom theme, submissive male theme, cross dressing, and a caning.

This book will be followed by a second book about the twins lives when they leave home for college and move in with a dominate female while attending college. The second book should be available summer 2012.

The Third series, the SISSY MAID MISSY BAD BOY SERIES, covers over five years of the life of a young rich boy.

My story begins in;

THE BAD BOY AND HIS FRENCH MAIDS and continues in

THE BAD BOY AND HIS FRENCH MAIDS, Two and in

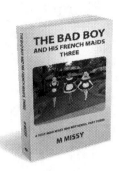

THE BAD BOY AND HIS FRENCH MAIDS,
Three

You learn that I was a rich teenager whose parents died in a plane crash and left me and my sister a two million dollar house and 10 million dollars. I then turned three young girls into French maid whores, for financial reasons and or immigration reasons they allowed this to happen.

The story includes French maids, anal sex, oral sex, spankings, canings, whippings, strappings, domination and submission, corner time, and a great amount of humiliation, etc.

My delight in training and punishing these three young women into submission eventually leads down a path that I wished that I never traveled.

In;

THE BAD BOY GETS PUNISHED,
and in

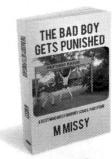

THE BAD BOYS GETS PUNISHED,
Two

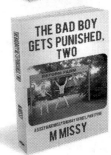

Where you will learn of the high price
I paid for abusing two of my three French
maids as I myself was punished and abused
and then turned into a sissy maid to serve
for those that I abused.

In;

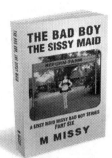

THE BAD BOY, THE SISSY MAID
and

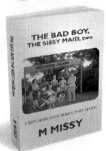

THE BAD BOY, THE SISSY MAID,
Two, and

THE BAD BOY, THE SISSY MAID,
Three, and

THE BAD BOY AND THE SISSY MAID,
Four, and

THE BAD BOY AND THE SISSY MAID,
five, and

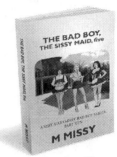

THE BAD BOY AND THE SISSY MAID,
six

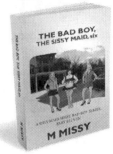

You learn about missy's 18 months of being
the sissy maid for the family that missy
once ruled over when he/she was the BOSS of
the house that she now maids for.

Missy's   life   continues   to   include
anal sex, oral sex, spankings, canings,
whippings,   strappings,   domination   and
submission, corner time, and a great amount
of humiliation, etc. to Missy.

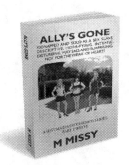

Next is ALLY'S GONE !!!!!!!!!!!

ALLY, one of missy's young beautiful Mistresses was kidnapped by the MOB in Venice, Italy while she was on vacation.

SLAVERY IS ALIVE AND WELL
SO, WHY DOES NO ONE REALLY CARE?

The Trafficking of human beings for prostitution, sexual slavery, and forced labor is the fastest growing criminal enterprise in the world. It is bigger than illegal drugs and illegal weapons in both size and scope. (According to "FREE THE SLAVES", a nonprofit human right organization)

It is almost a 20 billion dollar industry with victims totaling more than 25 million slaves. There are more people in slavery today that at any other time in history.

This story in just one story concerning kidnapping and sexual slavery.

However, this story is a unique look inside the brutal world of organized crime dealing with the kidnapping, the training, and the abuse of kidnapped victims from the inside.

You may and hopefully will find the contents of this book to be both sad and disturbing. But, it really happens, everyday, in one form of another, even here in the United States where it is estimated that between 50,000 and 100,000 boys and girls and young women are being held as sexual slaves every year.

Why is no one finding them? The real answer, except for a few, it is because no one is looking for them.

This book, although fictional, focuses on one group of kidnappers as discovered by this books special character, Missy. Because of Missy's special talents she was able to infiltrate the inner workings of the Mob to be able to share what she saw and experienced. But, did it cost Missy her life?

It's a tale that may disgust you as it is downright horrible. You may need a strong stomach to read what Missy saw and experienced.

But, don't think for one minute it could not happen to your daughter or a young woman you may know.

Later, in; THE TRUTH WILL SET YOU FREE

Sissy maid missy's life continues with his new wife Cally as everyone in the family tries to recover from the emotional turmoil of Ally's kidnapping, those horrible four days in Venice Italy with missy's heroic saving of Ally, Suzy, and 36 other girl from the hands of the Russian Mob.

However, missy's expectation of life returning to normal was not turning out as well as missy had hoped and expected as it seemed that every week there was one more problem confronting a family member or a friend.

Cally and Ally now saw missy as a hero and not a sissy maid. Missy did not want her life to change and needed to change their minds.

Cally's father, Steve, was drinking again. Cally needed to step in and fix that problem once and for all.

Mindy's new boyfriend took out his unhappiness on Mindy's face. No one, and missy meant no one, was going to hit a member of her family without being real sorry.

Toni's, Brother James was going bankrupt as he was cheated out of $50,000.00 by some dishonest management company. Cally was not going to allow someone to cheat Toni's brother, even if it was James.

Then there was the big murder case. Cally and missy were asked to help Rick, of the Reform Farm, when Rick was arrested for murder. All the evidence said that Rick did murder Jerry.

However, Cally and missy did believe Rick when he said he was home alone sleeping. This was the biggest mystery of Cally's and missy's life. Would the truth set Rick Free??????????

Towards the end of the trial, even missy was losing faith as they just could not find a way of defending Rick.

Then Cally told missy that missy was smart enough to figure it all out and to make Cally proud of her. MISSY, MAKE ME PROUD OF YOU!!!!

Was that enough, to get missy to find the truth, to set Rick free?????

The sissy maid missy bad boy series continues later summer.

A continuing series of special, good and bad, characters.

By, m missy